Sugar Spinelli's Little Instruction Book

I like surprises as much as the next gal, but the news about Adam Harper is more of a shock than a surprise. Still, I can't discount the source—she's Lightning Creek's most reliable gossip. And her latest juicy tidbit is spreading faster than a brush fire.

So why is Katie O'Hara staring at him as if he's the answer to her prayers? Surely she's not planning to bid on him? Didn't anyone warn her about Adam's little secret? Of course, Katie's got a few secrets of her own. Wait until I tell Ducky....

Dear Reader,

We just knew you wouldn't want to miss the news event that has all of Wyoming abuzz! There's a herd of eligible bachelors on their way to Lightning Creek—and they're all for sale!

Cowboy, park ranger, rancher, P.I.—they all grew up at Lost Springs Ranch, and every one of these mavericks has his price, so long as the money's going to help keep Lost Springs afloat.

The auction is about to begin! Young and old, every woman in the state wants in on the action, so pony up some cash and join the fun. The man of your dreams might just be up for grabs!

Marsha Zinberg
Editorial Coordinator, HEART OF THE WEST

It Happened One Weekend
Kristin Gabriel

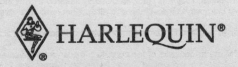

HARLEQUIN®

TORONTO • NEW YORK • LONDON
AMSTERDAM • PARIS • SYDNEY • HAMBURG
STOCKHOLM • ATHENS • TOKYO • MILAN • MADRID
PRAGUE • WARSAW • BUDAPEST • AUCKLAND

Kristin Gabriel is acknowledged as the author of this work.

ISBN 0-373-51156-6

IT HAPPENED ONE WEEKEND

Copyright © 1999 by Harlequin Books S.A.

Visit us at www.eHarlequin.com

Printed in U.S.A.

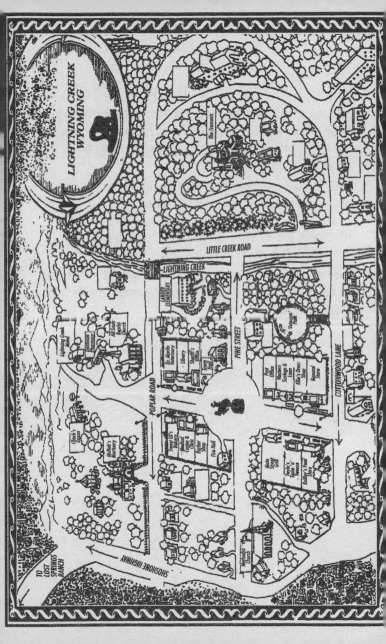

A Note from the Author

Can one weekend change your life forever? It happens to Katie O'Hara and her bachelor, Adam Harper. After a bumpy start, they set out for a romantic weekend—and find a few surprises along the way.

One of those surprises is Wiley, a pesky coyote pup who becomes an unlikely matchmaker. Living in farm country, I see (and hear!) coyotes on a regular basis. In fact, I developed the idea for Wiley as I lay in bed one night listening to the coyotes' moonlight serenade.

Ever take a coyote along on a date? Adam and Katie will never be the same. So sit back and enjoy *It Happened One Weekend.*

Kristin Gabriel

For Bruce, Matt, Jenny and Chelsea.
Thanks for your never-ending support
and cheerful patience.

CHAPTER ONE

"HOW MUCH POISON should I put in the beans?"

"Two heaping tablespoons," Katie O'Hara quipped, wiping her damp forehead with the back of her hand. She was hot and tired and ready for a break.

Marge Olson, a fellow waitress with forty years under her apron, frowned at the pot in front of her. "The recipe calls for three."

"I know," Katie replied, "but I already added some to the barbecue sauce."

The cowboy standing in the serving line grinned. "That's a joke, right?"

"Maybe," Katie teased, then dished up another plate of ribs, beans and coleslaw. She surveyed the crowd of customers in the pavilion without breaking her assembly-line rhythm. "Why did the Roadkill Grill ever agree to serve barbecue at this bachelor auction?"

"Publicity," Marge replied. "Our tightwad boss thinks the Roadkill will get a free plug in the *Gazette* when we both drop dead of hickory-smoke inhalation."

Katie waved away a pesky fly as perspiration trickled down the back of her dress. After slaving over a hot barbecue pit all afternoon, she should demand double pay for this duty.

Especially since she needed the money so desperately.

She handed a heavily laden plate to a waiting cowboy. He gave her a killer smile and a tip of his cowboy hat before sauntering off.

"That one's a heartbreaker," Marge observed, arching a thickly drawn brow.

"He certainly is." Katie nodded toward the tip jar filled with dollar bills and an assortment of change. "He stiffed us. What am I doing wrong?"

Marge laughed. "Nothing, hon. When you've been around as long as I have, you learn some men are handsome, some men are cheap, and some men are both."

Katie blew a stray wisp of hair out of her face, then let her gaze wander over the crowded grounds of the Lost Springs Ranch for Boys. "Well, there's sure no shortage of handsome men here."

Alumni of the ranch were gathered from all over the country to participate in the bachelor auction fund-raiser. Many of them had already been through the barbecue line, and their assessing glances had made Katie all too aware of her faded blue denim dress and the barbecue sauce smeared across the front of her white apron. The spicy red sauce matched the color of her sun-kissed nose and cheeks. Wisps of auburn hair had escaped her hairnet and hung in limp curls around her face.

"We're about out of beans," Marge informed her, moving from behind the table. "I'll have to go to the truck and grab a couple of cans. Can you handle it here?"

"Sure." Katie bent to pry the lid off a tub of coleslaw. It was difficult, because her left hand still hadn't fully healed since the car accident. She finally got the lid loose, gave the creamy salad a quick stir, then filled another paper plate with barbecue and salad. Slightly breathless from her effort, she pushed it into a lean, outstretched hand.

"Will you marry me?"

She looked up, startled by the deep voice of the man standing across the serving table. His blue eyes matched the wide Wyoming sky.

She took a deep breath. "What did you say?"

"I asked you to marry me." The stranger smiled at her, looking tall and cool and gorgeous. "Although I realize we haven't even been introduced yet. What's your name?"

She hesitated. "Katie. Katie O'Hara."

"I'm Adam Harper, and this is my third helping of barbecue." He held up his plate. "They say the way to a man's heart is through his stomach and, lady, I'm in love."

She swallowed, unnerved by the sexy dimple in his right cheek. "I'll tell Ernie you said so."

"Who's Ernie?"

"The cook. He's not married, either, so you may be in luck."

He frowned. "That puts a definite damper on my honeymoon fantasies. I pictured you and me and a big bottle of barbecue sauce."

She blushed, still not used to flirting with the customers. Marge was a pro at the waitress game and had the generous tips to prove it. But after six weeks on the job, Katie still couldn't handle a simple flirtation. So she fell back on one of her favorite lines from her favorite book. "You, sir, are no gentleman."

"While you, ma'am, are the prettiest lady here."

The statement was so ridiculous it made her laugh. "Which do you think does more for me, the apron or the hairnet?"

"Definitely the hairnet."

She patted her confined curls. "Well, then, I may just have to rethink that marriage proposal after all."

Marge arrived at the serving table before he could reply. "Sorry, I took so long," she said, an industrial-size can of beans tucked under each arm.

Adam Harper winked at Katie, stuffed a bill into the tip jar, then walked away.

"Oh, my," Marge exclaimed with a tilt of her jet black beehive. "That is the most perfect butt I've ever seen."

Katie forced herself to look away. Her heart still skittered from their encounter. Or maybe it was the sight of the twenty-dollar bill he'd casually stuck into the tip jar. "Really? I didn't notice."

"Then you've been out in the sun too long." Marge picked up a can opener. "Or maybe without a man too long."

Katie began filling plates again. "I don't need a man." That was an understatement. Her life was complicated enough without adding a man to the mix.

"I don't *need* one, either, but they sure can be fun to have around." Marge tipped the open can of beans into a serving pan. "Guess who I saw?"

"Who?"

"None other than champion bull rider Cody Davis. I'd give anything to hang that man's buckle over my bed."

Katie smiled to herself. Marge's weakness for rodeo men was second only to her reputation as Lightning Creek's unofficial news source. She served up fresh gossip with the morning coffee every day at the Roadkill Grill. "I thought you didn't like them that young."

"True, but a little fantasy never hurts now and then." Marge tossed the empty can into the Dumpster. "Hope nobody minds eating their beans cold."

Katie looked up, surprised to see the long line had suddenly dissipated. "I don't think we'll have to worry about it. Looks like the auction is about to begin."

Marge wiped her hands on a wet dishrag, then pulled a glossy catalog out of her back pocket. "I picked up one of the brochures so we can join in the fun. I'll bet we can even find a man for you in here."

Katie laughed, wiping her hands on her apron. "I don't think my tips at the Roadkill will quite cover the cost of one of these bachelors."

"Nonsense. Where there's a will, there's a way." Marge flipped through the bachelor brochure. "Oooh, look at this one. I wonder what's hidden under *his* apron."

Katie couldn't help but take a peek at the scantily clad chef. "Not bad."

Marge snorted. "Not bad? Girl, you need your head examined."

Katie winced. She'd had her head examined several times since the accident two months ago. The last specialist had concurred with her previous doctors.

I can't find any organic explanation for your condition, Ms. O'Hara. Perhaps the head injury you sustained is to blame. Or perhaps it's psychosomatic. There could be a reason you don't want to remember your past.

"How about this one?" Marge shoved the catalog under Katie's nose. "Did you ever see such muscles on a man?"

Katie shrugged. She honestly didn't know. She didn't remember anything of her life before the accident. Or anyone. Even more odd, no one seemed to remember her. She was a stranger to everyone on staff at the Converse County Hospital. A report of the accident had circulated in the area newspapers, but no one had come forward to claim her.

She'd been driving a brand new Ford Taurus along Shoshone Highway. According to the sheriff's report, Katie was found unconscious several feet from the wrecked, burning car. Fire had consumed everything, including the registration papers and the contents of her purse and overnight bag.

The only clue to her identity was an antique silver filigree ring. According to the emergency room nurse, it had been on the ring finger of her left hand. A wedding ring? But if so, where was her husband?

While she'd lain in the hospital for two weeks, the sheriff had searched his records for any missing-persons reports matching her description. But to no avail. She was a woman without a past. Without a family. Without a name.

So she'd chosen one of her own. Katie S. O'Hara. She'd picked it after reading *Gone With the Wind* three times while recuperating from her injuries. She admired Scarlett's spunk, her determination to achieve her heart's desire. Scarlett never gave up. And neither would Katie. Despite the fact that nothing and no one seemed familiar to her. Despite the fact that it would take months before she saved enough in tips and wages to hire a private detective to discover her real identity.

"You all right, hon?" Marge asked, her face pinched with concern. She knew about Katie's slow physical recovery from the accident, but not about the amnesia. As much as she liked Marge, Katie knew that telling her would be the same as announcing it in the Lightning Creek *Gazette*. For some reason, Katie didn't feel comfortable sharing her amnesia with other people. It made her feel too vulnerable. Too out of control. Sheriff Hatcher agreed with her decision. Especially since he wasn't entirely convinced the car crash had been an accident.

Katie forced a smile. "I'm fine."

"You're probably worn out. I should have hurried back here to help you instead of sight-seeing, no matter how sexy the sights." She led Katie to a lawn chair under a shady willow tree. "You just sit down here and rest a bit while I clean up." She laid the bachelor brochure in Katie's lap. "Do a little sight-seeing yourself."

Katie leaned back in the chair and kicked off her leather sandals, enjoying the feel of the silky grass beneath her bare feet. She flipped idly through the bachelor brochure as a warm breeze rustled the leaves above her. In the distance, she heard the squeak of a microphone through the P.A. system.

As she turned a page, her gaze fell on a picture of Robert Carter, a doctor from Denver. Her nose wrinkled involuntarily. He was incredibly handsome, but she'd had her fill of doctors. She flipped to the next page, and her heart stopped beating.

"Rodney." She breathed the word on a strangled gasp, her struggle for air bringing her out of the chair.

Marge hurried over to her. "Did you find a good one?"

Katie could only point to his picture. The wispy blond hair, just beginning to thin on top. The peach fuzz under his nose that barely passed for a mustache. The green eyes magnified by the thick lenses of his glasses.

"That one?" Marge asked in disbelief.

"Rodney Tate." Katie's voice sounded strange to her, so high and tight. She sat back and concentrated on breathing evenly and deeply. She couldn't fall apart now. Not when she was so close to getting her life back.

She knew this man.

But how? Was Rodney Tate her lover? Her husband? Her accountant? She closed her eyes. What did it matter? Finally. *Finally* a memory had surfaced in her mist-shrouded mind. After two long months she remembered someone. Right now it was only a face. A name. But it was the first step toward rediscovering herself.

Marge took the brochure out of her hands. "You're getting this excited over a fellow named Rodney? Honey, it has been a long time for you, hasn't it?" She pulled her bifocals out of her apron pocket to read his bio. "Rodney Tate. Thirty-one years old. Computer nerd."

Katie sat up and grabbed the catalog. "It doesn't say that."

"Maybe not, but just look at his picture. Have you taken a gander at some of the other men in here?"

"No. I just turned to his picture. It must have been…fate."

"You *have* been in the sun too long." Marge pushed her back into the chair. "Browse through the rest of the merchandise, then let me know which one you want. We'll snag one of these eligible bachelors for you."

"Rodney Tate and every other man here is going to sell for thousands of dollars," Katie replied, nervously twisting the antique ring on her finger. Marge had advised her to switch the ring to her right hand in order to garner better tips from the male customers. It had worked, too. Only she didn't have anywhere near the amount needed to participate in the auction.

"Just leave it to me. If there's one thing Marge Olson knows, it's how to get a man."

While Marge went back to cleaning up, Katie's mind raced. She had to find him. She had to talk to him. Slipping on her sandals, she peered over at the rows of bachelors seated on the stage.

Frustrated by a knot of women blocking her view, she stood up and sidled around them for a closer look. This time her gaze fell on Adam Harper. He was gorgeous even from a distance. Thick, dark brown hair. High cheekbones. A square jaw. Katie turned away, perturbed at herself for getting sidetracked.

Until her memory returned, she was stuck in limbo. While she might have her own fantasies about an attractive man, she couldn't act on them.

For all she knew, she could be in a committed relationship. Or even married. Until she regained her past, she couldn't have a future.

Rodney Tate was the key. She had so many questions for him. But she still hadn't spotted him among the crowd of handsome faces. Doubts assailed her. What if they barely knew each other? What if they'd met so far back in the past, he couldn't remember her? What if he refused to talk to her? This man was here for the bachelor auction, not to be interrogated by a waitress.

Just then she spotted Rex Trowbridge, the director of the Lost Springs Ranch and a frequent customer at the Roadkill Grill. She flagged him down.

"Hey, Katie, is there a problem with the food?"

"Food?" She blinked, confused for a moment. "No, the food is fine. But you've got another problem, Rex. One of the bachelors is missing."

He glanced at his clipboard. "I'm pretty sure they've all checked in—"

"Rodney Tate," she interjected. "The auction is ready to start, and he's nowhere in sight. Maybe we should contact Sheriff Hatcher in case he got lost or had a flat tire...or worse."

"Whoa, there." Rex held up one hand. "I appreciate your concern, but there's no reason to panic. I know where to find Tate."

Her knees grew weak with relief. "Where?"

"At his estate in Montana. He called me a week ago to withdraw his name from the auction. Tate just got engaged, and it seems his fiancée doesn't want to share him with another woman."

"I don't believe it," she whispered. *Rodney Tate was a no-show.* And now there was no chance of asking him anything. She glanced at his picture in the bachelor brochure, and the sense of recognition that swept over her grew even stronger.

"We were disappointed, too. But he did volunteer another bachelor to take his place."

"Great," she said numbly.

"Actually, I was surprised Harper agreed to it, since he declined our original invitation."

A pair of sky blue eyes flashed in her mind. "Did you say Harper?"

Rex glanced at his clipboard. "Adam Harper. I heard he's on his way to Tate's place in Montana to stand up as best man. Maybe filling in for him at the last minute is his wedding present. Lucky for us, huh?"

Katie could only nod, absorbing the impact of his words. She was vaguely aware of the amplified voice of the auctioneer and another, softer voice calling Rex away. She shook herself. *Get a grip, O'Hara.* She couldn't let this opportunity slip away. It might be her only chance to get her memory back. To get her *life* back.

As she watched the first bachelor sell for an obscene amount of money, Katie asked herself what Scarlett O'Hara would do in this situation. The answer seemed as obvious as it was impossible.

She had to buy Adam Harper.

ADAM HARPER liked women. Especially a woman like Katie O'Hara. She was exactly his type. Sexy and sassy. Tall and temporary. And smart enough to take his flip marriage proposal as a joke. He couldn't imagine committing to any woman for the rest of his life, although a weekend sounded just about right. He sat among the other Lost Springs alumni in the arena, watching as the current bachelor on the block preened and flexed his biceps for the adoring female crowd.

"This is a nightmare," muttered the man seated next to him.

Adam smiled. "Hey, this is my dream come true. A weekend fling with a willing woman—no strings attached."

"I guess I can't argue with that," the man replied grudgingly.

"The only downside," Adam continued, "is that the buyer gets to choose where and when. I prefer to be the one calling the shots."

"As I recall, your best shot was a mean left hook."

Adam glanced at the man, then did a double take. "Lydell?"

"That's right," Luke Lydell replied, extending his hand. "You haven't changed a bit, Harper."

Adam shook his hand with a firm grasp. "Should I take that as a compliment or an insult?"

Luke laughed. "Take it as a compliment. As I remember it, the last guy who insulted you walked away with quite a shiner."

"That was a long time ago."

"True enough," Luke agreed, then settled back in his folding chair. "So what are you up to now?"

"I own half of a business software company called ExecTec."

Max whistled low. "Impressive. I've heard ExecTec is a hot new prospect on the stock market. So do you spend all day in front of a computer screen?"

"Actually I run the security division. Rodney Tate owns the other half of the company. He's in charge of software development."

Luke nodded. "I remember Tate. So he's the brains and you're the brawn?"

"Something like that." Adam didn't bother to add that he managed all the accounts, marketing and personnel. Or that for the last couple of months his attention had been focused on a possible security leak. Piracy was rampant in the software business, and it was his job to protect the interests of ExecTec.

His prime suspect was a leggy redhead wearing dark sunglasses. He'd never seen her himself, but that was the description the doorman at his apartment building had given after he caught her trying to wrangle her way into Adam's penthouse.

Since then Adam had discovered other suspicious activity, including evidence of someone gaining access to confidential company personnel files. Not enough to go to the police with yet, but enough to make him determined to track this woman down and press charges, if possible.

He shifted in his chair, impatient to leave Lost Springs behind so he could start his search. But then, he'd always been impatient to leave Lost Springs. He'd been ten years old when his mother and stepfather had placed him at the boys' ranch, claiming they couldn't handle him anymore. Adam had never liked his stepfather, a harsh, cold man who had no patience with children. He'd certainly had no sympathy for Adam, who was still deeply troubled after the recent death of his beloved father.

So Adam had spent more and more time on his own, running with a group of older, street-tough boys. After a series of minor scrapes with the law, his stepfather had demanded Adam's mother make a choice between her son and her husband.

She'd made it.

Shortly thereafter, Adam had found himself dumped off at Lost Springs. He'd gotten into a fight the first day, protecting another new boy, a scrawny nerd named Rodney who was crying his eyes out over the recent death of his parents. When one of the older boys started heckling the nerd, Adam had punched him in the mouth. Despite his own tough hide, he couldn't stand to see anyone pick on the weak. He'd earned a broken nose for his trouble. And a case of hero worship from the nerd. He'd also been pegged as a troublemaker that day and had done his best to live up to his reputation.

He smiled to himself, remembering some of the more scandalous escapades of his youth. No doubt the good folks of Lightning Creek had breathed a sigh of relief when Adam Harper had finally left town.

"Hey, looks like you're up, Harper," Luke said, nodding toward the dais.

Adam rose to his feet as the auctioneer called his name, aware that every eye in the arena was on him. The variety of women here fascinated him. Young and old. Short and tall. Blondes, brunettes and redheads. A wry smile tipped up his mouth as his pulse quickened with anticipation. There was something almost tantalizing about pairing up with a perfect stranger. Especially one who paid thousands of dollars to spend a weekend with you.

But instead of the wolf whistles and hoots that had greeted some of the previous bachelors, Adam's appearance caused an odd murmuring to sweep through the crowd.

The auctioneer cleared his throat. "Ladies, we've got a mystery bachelor here. Adam Harper is one of our bonus bachelors, so you won't find him listed in the brochure." He pointed to Adam. "If you like surprises, this is just the man for you."

A nervous titter rippled through the audience.

"Shall we start the bidding at five hundred dollars?"

Adam's gaze scanned the crowd while he waited for the women to start haggling over him. He spotted Katie O'Hara near the front row, clutching a jelly jar to her chest. She stood next to her partner-in-barbecue, a sharp-eyed harridan with mile-high hair and a cigarette dangling from her crimson lips. The harridan blew a smoke ring at him and winked.

He didn't want to even think about landing in her clutches for a weekend. But Adam soon realized he didn't need to worry about it. The harridan wasn't bidding on him.

Nobody was bidding on him.

"Do I hear a bid of four hundred dollars?" the auctioneer boomed. "Who'll give me four hundred?"

Nobody raised a hand. A group of women began whispering together in the front row. For a moment, Adam thought they were pooling their money to buy him—until he saw one of them dealing out a deck of cards. Then he wondered if they were going to let the high card win him, until one of them cried, "Go fish."

"Do I hear three hundred?" the auctioneer called, clearly as puzzled as Adam by this sudden lull in the proceedings. "C'mon, ladies, any bachelor is a steal at that price."

Sweat broke out on his forehead. The last bachelor had just sold for over seven *thousand* dollars. What in the hell was the problem?

The auctioneer waved Adam to the podium. "Maybe we just need a few clues about our mystery bachelor to whet their appetites."

Adam smiled, his lips stiff. Just his luck. All the previous bachelors had to do was stand on the dais like beefcake on the hoof.

The auctioneer tipped up his cowboy hat far enough to scratch his pale forehead. "Well, sir, we all know you grew up right here at Lost Springs. Where do you live now?"

"Chicago." His clipped reply echoed over the loudspeaker.

"And what do you do there?"

"I run the security division for a computer software company," he said, keeping it short and simple.

"Security? Is that right?" The auctioneer chuckled. "So any of these ladies will be safe with you?"

"Perfectly safe," he affirmed.

A smattering of laughter arose from the crowd.

"Now we're getting 'em warmed up," the auctioneer said under his breath. "All right, ladies, that's just enough to leave you wanting more."

Adam stepped away from the podium to face the scrutiny of the crowd once again.

The auctioneer cleared his throat. "Let's start the bidding at one hundred dollars and work our way up. Do I hear one hundred?"

The crowd began shuffling in the bleachers, obviously growing impatient. But nobody put him out of his misery by bidding on him. Adam ran a finger around his shirt collar. This was worse than the time his fraternity brothers had dared him to sing "Copacabana" at that Karaoke bar in Laramie.

Maybe he should have built himself up more. Mentioned his penthouse apartment on Chicago's North Shore. Or his kick-ass Dodge Durango with the turbo-charged engine and stereo CD player.

He just didn't understand it. Attracting women had never been his problem. Letting them down easy when they pushed for a commitment had always been the hard part of his relationships.

He saw Lindsay Duncan, the owner of the Lost Springs Ranch, rush over to consult with Rex Trowbridge. Thanks to Adam, their celebrated bachelor auction had just come to a grinding halt.

"Only one hundred dollars, ladies," the auctioneer pleaded. "Any bachelor is a bargain at that price."

He now knew the definition of an eternity. Adam closed his eyes, wanting this nightmare to end.

"Who will give me a bid?" cried the auctioneer, desperation straining his voice. "Any bid?"

"Forty-seven dollars and fifty-five cents!" cried a lone feminine voice.

Adam's eyes snapped open, but he was too late to identify his buyer. Everyone in the arena breathed a collective sigh of relief.

The auctioneer slammed his hammer down on the podium. "Sold!"

CHAPTER TWO

KATIE SCOOPED the last three coins out of the bottom of the jelly jar. "Forty-five...fifty...fifty-five." She counted aloud. "There." She shoved the pile of dollar bills and loose change across the table to settle her account. "Forty-seven dollars and fifty-five cents." It might not be much money compared to the thousands of dollars other women had spent today, but it was a fortune in her eyes. She still felt a twinge of guilt for letting Marge talk her into using all the money in the tip jar.

One of the auction officials began sorting through the heap of nickels, dimes and quarters on the table. "Thank you for your donation. I hope your bachelor makes all your dreams come true."

"Me, too," Katie murmured as she turned to look for the man who could change her life. Everything was working out perfectly. She'd been a little worried about coming up with enough money to buy a bachelor as sexy as Adam Harper, but a few well chosen words via Marge's grapevine had solved that little problem.

Katie headed toward the pavilion to search for her bachelor. As she crossed the wide gravel drive, a battered green pickup pulled up beside her. Sam Duncan switched off the ignition, then leaned out the window, his battered cowboy hat shading his grizzled face. After working at the Lost Springs Ranch for more than forty years, Sam was mostly retired now and a daily customer at the Roadkill Grill.

"Hey, Katie, can I give you a lift back into town?"

"No, thanks, Sam. But you can answer a question for me." She stepped toward the pickup. "Do you remember Adam Harper?"

Sam rested his wrist atop the steering wheel. "Sure do. Harper showed up here in the summer of seventy-nine. His folks barely slowed their car down long enough to drop him off."

Katie leaned against the driver's door of the pickup. "You mean he wasn't an orphan?"

"Nope. Not all the boys at the ranch come here as orphans. A few get into trouble with the law or become too much for their parents to handle. Lost Springs is their last chance to set themselves straight."

"And Adam was one of them," Katie said thoughtfully.

Sam nodded. "Harper wasn't even a teenager yet when he arrived here, but he already had a juvenile record and a big chip on his shoulder."

A record? Did that mean he was dangerous? For the first time it occurred to her that she was about to take off to parts unknown with a total stranger. She'd been so worried about finding her past, she hadn't given any consideration to taking care of herself in the present.

"Why all the questions, Katie?"

"I bought Adam Harper at the auction today." She took a deep breath. "Now I'm wondering if I've made a big mistake. Do you think he might be dangerous?''

He chuckled. ''Well, now, I haven't seen Harper for over twenty years. But as I remember it, the only thing a woman had to fear from him was a broken heart.''

She breathed a sigh of relief. ''A heartbreaker I can handle. Especially since I'm not planning to let him anywhere near mine.''

Sam drew his bushy gray brows together. ''Then why did you bid on him?''

''Call it an impulse buy,'' she replied. ''Besides, we'll only be together for a weekend.'' *If that long.* ''I just want to have a good time.''

''Then Harper is definitely your man. He used to have such a good time with the ladies that he still holds the record for breaking curfew.''

The affection she heard in the old man's voice relieved the last of her anxieties. ''Then it sounds like I won't suffer from buyer's remorse. I'll give you a full report when I get back to town.''

''Just tell Marge,'' he quipped. ''Then everybody will know the whole story inside an hour.''

She laughed as she pushed away from the pickup. ''See ya, Sam,'' she said, waving as he drove off. He left a cloud of dust in his wake. When the dust cleared, she spotted her bachelor near the concession stand.

She hovered on the edge of the pavilion, watching Adam sip beer out of a frosty mug. His white shirt, damp with perspiration, molded against his back. It outlined his broad shoulders, the taut muscles flexing as he raised the beer mug to his mouth.

He was gorgeous and he was all hers. Temporarily, anyway. Only how could she talk him into taking her to Montana with him? More important, how could she talk him *out* of his barbecue-sauce fantasy?

She twisted the ring on her finger, thinking up one lame excuse after another. Barbecue sauce gave her hives. She didn't like to eat between meals. Her mother had told her never to have sex unless her partner wore a condiment.

The last one didn't even make sense, although it did provoke an unbidden image of Adam slathered in barbecue sauce. A naked Adam. A smiling, naked Adam. Katie shook herself. This was not helping. She'd deal with his fantasies later. First, she had to inform him that he had a date for the wedding.

As she walked up behind him, a wave of guilt hit her. She was using him. Using him to get to Rodney. It sounded selfish and desperate and very Scarlett O'Hara-like. Still, she rationalized to herself, she only wanted to use him for the weekend. And she had contributed to charity to do it.

Which didn't exactly make her a saint, but Melanie was a saint in *Gone With the Wind,* and look what happened to her. Her mind made up, Katie tapped Adam on the shoulder before she completely lost her nerve.

He turned around. "Oh, it's you." His mouth relaxed into a smile. "Taking a break?"

"Actually, I'm off for the entire weekend. Free to do…whatever." She held her breath, waiting for him to thank her for bidding on him.

"Then maybe you can answer a question for me." He took another long swallow of beer. "What kind of cheapskate would pay bargain-basement prices for a charitable cause?''

Okay, so maybe he wasn't going to thank her. Especially since he didn't even seem to realize that he was talking to the cheapskate in question. How could he have missed her bid? She was the only interested woman in the arena. Nobody but Katie had wanted him, and the guy wasn't even grateful!

She tipped up her chin, stung by his remark. ''I wouldn't exactly call her a cheapskate.''

He shrugged. ''How about miser? Skinflint? Tightwad?''

''All right, I get your point,'' she said between clenched teeth. His opinion of her didn't matter, she reminded herself. All that mattered was meeting Rodney Tate. And the best way to get to Rodney was through Adam Harper.

Adam took another swig of his beer. ''I still can't believe I sold for a lousy forty-seven dollars.''

''And fifty-five cents,'' she reminded him.

He snorted. ''Right. Do you suppose she would accept a refund?''

Katie's mouth fell open. ''A refund? Why?''

''Because I'm a busy man. I only agreed to participate in this auction to help out a friend.'' He lifted his beer mug to his lips. ''Some help I turned out to be.''

''Every penny counts.''

''Well, I'd say my buyer is definitely a penny-pincher. Which doesn't sound like my idea of a fun date. Now all I want to do is find her, buy her off and get the hell out of Wyoming.''

That was the last thing she wanted. He wasn't going anywhere without her. It was time to set her bachelor straight. She squared her shoulders. "I know where you can find her."

His gaze narrowed. "You know this woman?"

Now there was a trick question. She didn't know herself. Not yet. That's why she had to convince him to go through with his end of the bachelor auction bargain.

His expression grew wary. "Don't tell me the bidder is…" His voice trailed off as his gaze focused over her shoulder. "Oh, no."

She turned around to see Marge striding purposefully toward them, a cigarette dangling from one corner of her mouth. Her short pink dress revealed a pair of knobby knees and a network of varicose veins on her bony legs. She'd been widowed three times and claimed she wouldn't marry again until she found a man lively enough to keep up with her. She ogled Adam like he was the main dish on a beefcake buffet.

"This is what I call a man," Marge announced when she reached them. She slowly circled Adam, looking him up and down. "Definitely money well spent. He's USDA Prime."

"Excuse me, Miss…" he began.

"Olson," she told him with a toothy smile. "But you can call me Marge."

He tentatively held out his hand. "Nice to meet you, Marge."

She grabbed it, pumping it up and down. "Believe me, the pleasure is all mine." Then her hand snaked up his arm and squeezed his biceps. "Lean and strong. Just the way I like 'em."

Adam took a step back, almost bumping into Katie. "Listen, Marge, about the auction…"

She took a step closer to him. "I expect plenty of romance for my money. A weekend a lady will never forget." She lowered her voice an octave as she leaned into him. "Are you up to it, Harper?"

Katie had to give him credit, he stood his ground.

"I'll do my best," Adam replied.

Marge slapped him on the butt. "That's all I want. Your best. Your very best." She cackled, then hailed a bowlegged cowboy at the other end of the pavilion.

Adam watched Marge sashay away, then turned to Katie, his expression puzzled. "What just happened here?"

Katie smiled. "I'd say you just received Marge's unique seal of approval."

"I'm not going to get out of this, am I?"

"I can almost guarantee it."

Without another word, Adam turned and headed for the concession stand. He traded his empty beer mug for a full one brimming with foam on the top. Katie followed him, wondering how much time she'd have to prepare for their trip. She needed to pack and change out of her dress into comfortable traveling clothes.

He downed half of his beer before speaking again. "Do you think she'd accept two hundred dollars to forget all about me?"

"Marge didn't buy you," Katie said, steeling herself for his reaction. "I did."

Adam slowly turned to look at her. "*You* bought me?"

Katie nodded, willing herself to brazen her way through this. "That's right."

"Then why did Marge have her hands all over me?"

"Because I used all the tips from the tip jar to buy you, including her half. I guess she wanted to make certain we got our money's worth."

He stared at her until Katie began to feel self-conscious. She smoothed her dress, then realized she still wore her barbecue-stained apron. And her hairnet. She plucked the hairnet off her head, crumpling it in her hands. "I feel a little like Cinderella. Only I'm on my way to a wedding instead of a ball."

"I think there's been a mistake," he said, stepping away from her. "A big mistake. I'm not your Prince Charming."

"There's no mistake. You're all mine, Adam."

He placed his hands on her shoulders. "Katie, I like you. I really do."

"I like you, too."

"But I have no intention of marrying you. Or anyone. Ever. That marriage proposal earlier was just a joke. Obviously not a very good one, but still a joke." He spoke very slowly, enunciating each word. "There will be no wedding."

She blinked at him. "I know that. I didn't mean *our* wedding." The last thing she needed on top of all her other problems was a possible bigamy charge. "I meant Rodney Tate's wedding."

His hands dropped from her shoulders. "What?"

"I want our weekend together to start right away. I can be ready to go in twenty minutes."

"Wait a minute. You know Rodney?"

Another trick question. "Well, I know he lives in Montana, and I've always wanted to go there." Along with every other state in the union. Especially since she couldn't remember seeing any place outside of Lightning Creek.

"Montana looks like Wyoming, only bigger. Does Acapulco appeal to you?"

"Well, sure..."

"Me, too." His smile returned, bringing that unexpected dimple with it this time. "We'll spend our weekend together there." His smile widened. "I'll even bring the barbecue sauce."

Katie didn't tell him she had no intention of fulfilling his fantasy. Or putting off their weekend. But what could she tell him? *I have amnesia and I'd like to tag along with you to this wedding, because I think I recognize the groom.* It sounded preposterous even to her.

"So what weekend looks good on your calendar?" he asked.

"This weekend."

He shook his head. "I already told you, that doesn't work for me. How about a month from now?"

"You don't understand." She moistened her dry lips with her tongue. "It has to be this weekend. I'm not open to negotiations."

"I've got plans."

"I know," she replied, smiling at him, willing him to go along with her scheme. "I love weddings."

He frowned. "Sorry, Katie, but this weekend just doesn't work for me. Besides, you won't know anyone there."

She sincerely hoped that wasn't true. "I'll know you. I get to pick the weekend, and this is the one I want."

He set his jaw. "No."

"It's in the bachelor auction rules," she insisted. "The buyer gets to select the weekend of her choice." She was bluffing. She hadn't even paid attention to the rules.

"Then I guess our deal is off." He reached into his back pocket and pulled out his wallet. "I'll be happy to reimburse you."

She folded her arms across her chest. "I don't want your money, Adam. I want you."

He held out several bills. "One hundred dollars to forget the whole thing."

She scowled at him. "You were going to offer Marge two hundred."

"All right, two hundred."

"No, thank you."

A muscle knotted his jaw as he pulled out another bill. "Three hundred."

She pressed her lips together and shook her head.

"Four hundred?"

She began tapping her foot, impatiently waiting for him to realize she meant business.

He folded his arms. "Four hundred dollars is my final offer."

"Good, then we can discuss our travel arrangements. Do you plan to fly or drive to Montana?"

"Fly," he replied. "Alone."

She heaved a sigh of exasperation. "I thought we'd already settled this."

"Five hundred," he said. "Or a trip to Acapulco. Take it or leave it."

"I'll take Acapulco," she said evenly, "by way of Montana."

With a grunt of irritation, he grasped her elbow

and pulled her away from the crowded pavilion. "Look, I'm not taking you to Montana. I have some serious business matters to handle there."

"I promise to stay out of your way."

He stopped under the shade of a towering oak tree, then turned to face her. "Rodney Tate lives on an isolated estate in the middle of nowhere. Butte is the nearest town, and it's ninety miles away."

"It sounds perfect," she insisted.

"It will be boring as hell." He stepped closer to her. "Wouldn't you rather spend a weekend together in Acapulco?" His deep voice grew husky. "We could drink margaritas while we wallow in barbecue sauce."

She closed her eyes to shut out the temptation of his handsome face. "I've always wanted to see Butte."

He threw up his hands. "All right. Have it your way. But I think you're *nuts* to pass up Acapulco."

The technical term for her mental state was psychogenic amnesia, but she had no intention of telling him that. He'd use it as the perfect excuse to leave her high and dry in Lightning Creek. *Rodney Tate, here I come.*

He pulled a business card out of his shirt pocket and handed it to her. "Give me a call in a month and we'll make plans."

"A month?" She faltered.

"You want to go to Montana, then I'll take you to Montana." He handed her his business card. "But not this weekend."

Then he was gone.

Her jaw dropped as he stalked away, taking his

arrogant attitude and his perfect butt with him.

Adam Harper was leaving without her.

ADAM SAT wedged in the driver's seat of his rental car, a small hatchback with too many miles and a leak in the muffler. Now he knew why it had been the last car left in the rental lot when he'd arrived in Casper this morning.

He'd just spent the last hour coaxing the stubborn car into starting for him. From the roar of the engine and the black smoke emanating from the exhaust pipe, he'd guess the transmission was going.

At least he was finally on his way. More than ready to put his old and new memories of Lost Springs behind him. Especially his most recent memory of a sexy, determined waitress who wouldn't take no for an answer.

As the car bounced over the gravel drive leading from the ranch, he found himself hoping she'd take him up on his Acapulco offer. Something about Katie O'Hara intrigued him, and he'd welcome an opportunity to get to know her better.

Only not this weekend.

He needed to inform Rodney about the possible security leak and discuss their options. Then, as soon as the wedding was over, he'd begin his hunt for that mysterious redhead. When he found her, he intended to prosecute her to the full extent of the law. She'd be sorry she'd ever tangled with Adam Harper. He couldn't stand sneakiness or deceit, especially from a woman.

His grip on the steering wheel relaxed as the wide open gate to the Lost Springs Ranch came into view. Only a few more yards to go. Beyond it lay the majestic Wind River Range, the granite mountain peaks framed in a soft rainbow of colors by the setting sun.

The next moment, he saw a flash of pink directly in front of him. He slammed on the brakes, his heart hammering in his chest as the car slid to a stop, spitting gravel and dust in its wake. The engine choked and sputtered, then finally died.

Marge Olson stood in front of the bumper, hands on her hips and a smile on her face. Adam swallowed a groan. He'd been *so* close. He opened the driver's door, then maneuvered his long legs out of the compact car. As he worked the kinks out of his calf muscles, he envisioned the trip to the airport in Casper with his knees contorted to fit under the steering wheel.

"My first husband always said I had a face that could stop traffic," Marge said with a wink.

"I came this close to hitting you," Adam exclaimed, his thumb almost rubbing against his forefinger.

Marge pursed her lips. "You don't look like the type of man to hit a woman."

"I mean with my car," he explained through clenched teeth. "What the hell were you doing standing in the middle of the road? You're lucky the one thing that works on this pile of scrap metal is the brakes!" Adam forced himself to take a deep, calming breath. His gaze drifted to the front gate. Only a few more yards to freedom. He could hop in the car, gun the engine and leave Marge and all his bad memories behind. Only with his luck, the engine would die and he'd be stuck in Lightning Creek overnight.

He turned to Marge and managed a half smile.

"Look, I'm sorry I lost my temper. I've got a plane to catch, so I'm in a bit of a hurry."

She walked up to him, hooking her arm through his. "Well, I just wanted to catch you before you left."

He hoped she didn't mean that literally. "Why?"

"So I could apologize. Sometimes I come on a little too strong, although that's what my third husband liked best about me. He admired assertive women." She began to walk toward the parking lot, pulling Adam along with her. "Of course, he'd never actually married one before. He died on our honeymoon."

"I'm sorry," Adam said, trying hard not to imagine the circumstances of his death.

"I'm probably boring you."

"Not at all," he said politely, sneaking a glance at his watch.

She smiled at him, the gold cap on her front tooth gleaming in the sun. "You're such a nice young man. That's why I've decided to give you a little treat for the road."

He was almost afraid to ask. "Treat?"

She stopped near an old black pickup with a camper top parked in the corner of the lot. "Just follow me," she said, popping open the back door of the camper.

He hesitated. "Listen, Marge, I really do have to be going."

"This will only take a minute," she promised, then disappeared inside.

With a sigh of resignation, he followed her. The spicy aroma of barbecue hit him as soon as he entered the cramped camper. The walls were covered with cheap wood paneling and the floor with green indoor-outdoor carpeting. Boxes and serving dishes and an assortment of shiny utensils were neatly stacked on a makeshift counter.

Marge sidled her way through the crowded cabin to the compact refrigerator humming in the corner. She pulled out a large shoe box, the lid secured with a bright red ribbon. "Here you go," she said, handing it to him.

He took the box gingerly in his hands.

"What is it?"

"Just a little something to tide you over on your trip. Some leftover barbecue, a tub of coleslaw, and a man-size slice of the cherry pie I picked up at the church bake sale this morning." She nudged him in the ribs with her elbow. "You may even find a thermos bottle of my homemade cider in there. It packs quite a punch."

He was both surprised and touched. "You didn't have to go to all this trouble for me."

She grinned.

"Believe me, the pleasure is all mine."

On impulse, he leaned over to kiss her rouged cheek. "Thanks, Marge." Then he turned to go.

"Oh, by the way..." Her voice trailed off.

He looked at her over his shoulder, his hand on the aluminum doorknob. "Yes?"

She hesitated. "I just wanted to remind you that hardly anybody believes what they read in the newspapers anymore."

The statement was so odd, he couldn't let it go. Against his better judgment, he turned to face her. "Why should I need reassurance?"

She shrugged. "There were a few reporters milling about in the crowd today."

"So?"

"So...they may have happened to overhear some things not intended for their ears or their pencils." She wrinkled her forehead. "Although so many of them work on those laptop computers these days. You hardly see any journalists rely on a good old notepad and pencil. Where would the world be without electricity?"

"Laptops run on batteries," he said, still trying to decipher her cryptic comment about newspapers. Maybe he didn't want to know. Maybe he should just turn around and leave while he still had the chance.

Instead he tucked the box under his arm. "What are you trying to tell me, Marge? Or rather, not tell me?"

She cleared her throat. "I suppose you do deserve an explanation after what we put you through at the auction."

"We?"

"Katie and I. Although it was my idea," she hastened to add. "Now I just have to find a way to make it up to Lindsay."

Adam shifted the box in his arms, thoroughly confused. "Marge, what are you talking about?"

"I'm talking about arranging it so Katie could buy you for under fifty dollars. I know it was a little underhanded, but she really wanted you. Which was a big relief to me after I'd seen her first choice."

Her first choice? "Go on."

"Well, I just feel a little guilty because the boys

ranch could have made a lot more money off you, with your butt and all, if I hadn't interfered.''

Adam got a sinking feeling in the pit of his stomach. ''Exactly how did you interfere?''

She leaned against the counter. ''Just a few well-chosen words in the right ears. Rumors spread faster than a brushfire around here. Especially rumors about a sexy, handsome, single man like you.''

He closed his eyes. ''You told everyone I'm gay, didn't you?''

Marge snorted. ''Of course not. I'm much more creative, not to mention politically correct.''

He let out the breath he didn't know he'd been holding. The last thing his company needed was publicity about his sex life. ''Then what did you say?''

''I told them you were permanently impotent due to a tragic childhood accident involving a bucking horse and a fence post.''

The twilight zone. He'd crossed the Wyoming border and entered the twilight zone. Now he just had to find his way out before his life spiraled completely out of control.

''So that's why....'' His voice trailed off as all the pieces fell in to place.

''That's why nobody bid on you. Women like a challenge, but a weekend is hardly enough time to—''

''I get your point,'' he interjected. He should have listened to his instincts and left while he had the chance. He backed out of the camper. ''Well, I've really got to go now.''

''Don't worry,'' Marge called after him, ''those reporters didn't seem all that interested in the story.

I'm sure it will all be forgotten before you can say pass the Viagra.''

Adam sprinted to his car, jumped into the driver's seat and tossed the shoe box into the back. To his utter amazement the car started on the first try. He pulled out of the front gate, eager to put as many miles between him and Lost Springs as possible.

Unfortunately, the faulty transmission made it impossible to go over forty miles per hour. He'd have to take back roads to avoid being a traffic hazard on the highway. Which meant adding at least two hours to the trip. Gritting his teeth, Adam turned off Shoshone Highway and onto a county road.

After the first twenty minutes on the road, the red haze began to clear from his eyes. After forty minutes he loosened his death grip on the steering wheel. After sixty minutes he leaned back against the vinyl seat and breathed a long sigh of relief.

Then he heard somebody sneeze.

CHAPTER THREE

KATIE HELD her breath. Her entire body ached from her cramped position pressed against the hatchback of the small car. The musty blanket that covered her from head to toe made her itch everywhere. An hour ago, stowing away in Adam's car had seemed like a good idea. That was before she'd had time to imagine his reaction when he found her—which, judging by his startled exclamation, would be sooner rather than later.

She heard the squeal of the brakes and the crunch of gravel, bracing herself against Adam's leather suitcase as the car lurched to a stop. Next came the sound of the driver's door opening, then slamming shut. She inched the blanket down to her chin just as the hatchback popped open.

Adam glared at her. "What the hell do you think you're doing?"

"Surprise," she said weakly. Even in the shadowy light of dusk she could tell he wasn't happy to see her. In fact, he looked furious.

"I don't like surprises," he said through clenched teeth. "How did you get in here?"

She swallowed. "I sort of snuck in while you were talking to Marge."

His jaw dropped. "It was all a setup, wasn't it?

That barbecue care package was just a ploy so you could stow away in my car!''

"Marge knew we had a long trip ahead of us and she wanted to make sure we didn't go hungry."

He narrowed his eyes. "You are *not* coming with me to Montana."

She raised herself on her elbows. "Look, we're already on our way, so why not get our weekend over with? Then you'll never have to see me again." She lay back down and closed her eyes. "You won't even know I'm here."

"That's because you won't be." He grabbed the shoe box out of the back seat, then he grabbed Katie.

She let out a small shriek as he hauled her up, blanket and all, into his arms. Her heart pounded as he cradled her tightly against his broad chest. "Where are you taking me?"

"Get it through that pretty head of yours once and for all, Miss O'Hara. I'm not taking you anywhere."

He turned away from the car and carried her off the gravel road and into an empty field. "You've caused me enough trouble for one day with that ridiculous impotency rumor."

Did he intend to disprove it to her? Trepidation mingled with anticipation as he carried her toward a lone, leafless tree, its thick, blackened trunk split down the middle.

He carried her as if she weighed almost nothing at all, and an awareness of his physical strength tingled through her. For a brief moment she allowed herself to imagine a weekend with Adam that involved no ulterior motives. Just the two of them, enjoying each other instead of at odds with each other. The image ended abruptly when he dumped her unceremoniously into the tall sagebrush.

"Ow!" she cried as something small and sharp jabbed her in the backside. She reached down and pulled out a thorn. "You dropped me in a patch of cockleburs!"

He arched an eyebrow. "May I be of assistance?"

"No," she retorted, determined to suffer in silence. She certainly wouldn't give him the satisfaction of pulling cockleburs out of her behind.

He dropped the shoe box of leftover barbecue next to her. "Have a pleasant evening, Miss O'Hara." Then, without another word, he turned and walked toward the car.

"You can't just leave me here," she called to his retreating back. The blanket tangled around her legs as she struggled to stand up.

"Watch me," Adam shouted over his shoulder. Then he climbed into the car and eased it onto the road.

She watched in horrified disbelief as the car's red taillights grew smaller and smaller. He was leaving her. He was actually leaving her in the middle of nowhere. At night. Alone.

"Now what, Katie Scarlett?" she muttered, looking nervously around her. The last rays of sunlight shimmered in the horizon as night descended over the stark grasslands. No streetlights illumined the deserted gravel road, and somehow Katie instinctively knew she'd always been afraid of the dark.

Drawing the blanket closer around her, she stood huddled in the tall brush. An owl hooted in the distance. And closer, much closer, she heard the bone-chilling howl of a coyote.

ADAM COULDN'T FIND her anywhere.

He'd only driven five miles before he'd turned the car around. Just enough time to let his temper—and his body—cool off. Carrying her in his arms had been a big mistake. Especially since he'd been attracted to her from the first moment he saw her. She'd been soft and round in all the right places. Her light, alluring scent still clung to his clothes.

It was enough to make him seriously consider a cold shower. Not that he'd find a shower, or even indoor plumbing, in this remote area of Wyoming. He couldn't even find one tall, troublesome woman.

For the past twenty minutes, he'd walked the edge of the road, trying to find some sign of her. He'd left the headlights on to counter the enveloping darkness, but he'd gone far enough that they were only glowing pinpricks in the distance.

He turned and headed in the opposite direction. He never should have left her here alone. She didn't deserve that kind of treatment even if she had tricked him. The problem was he abhorred deception of any kind.

He'd learned his lesson about deceit early on from a woman who had meant everything to him. *We're going to take a tour of that boys' ranch,* his mother had said all those years ago, *just to see what it's like. Why don't you come along?*

She'd liked it so much she'd left him there. Of course, that had been her and his stepfather's plan all along. And Adam had foolishly accompanied them on the trip because he'd believed his mother. Trusted her. Loved her.

He shoved the memory out of his mind. All that mattered now was finding Katie. He scanned up and down both sides of the country road. No sign of her. Raw panic consumed him as a coyote howled in the distance.

"Please let me find her," he pleaded under his breath, walking faster. "Please let her be all right." If anything happened to her, he'd never forgive himself.

It was completely dark, with only a sliver of moon illuminating the night sky. Every horrific fate possible ran through his imagination. She could have been carried off by wild animals, or bitten by a rattlesnake, or abducted by aliens.

"Just let me find her," he pleaded under his breath. "I'll take her to Montana. I'll take her anywhere she wants to go."

He searched far north of the blackened tree, hoping to see some glimpse of her, frustrated by the darkness hampering his search. He threw back his head and shouted, "Katie! Katie, where are you?"

No reply. Nothing but the flap of birds' wings above him. A hawk soared in the night sky, hunting for prey. If only Adam had night vision. Or even a flashlight.

What now? Should he call the authorities? Organize a search party? He trudged through the endless stretch of pastureland. How could a woman just disappear? If he could find something, anything, to lead him in the right direction.

"Katie, where are you?" he called out in despair.

Then he heard it. A soft, distant voice carried on the wind. "I'm over here."

Relief flooded through him at the sound of her voice. She wasn't dead. *Yet.* After the turmoil she'd just put him through, he didn't know whether to kill her or kiss her. He ran toward the area her voice had come from, still unable to see her in the darkness. At last he could make out an amorphous shape, then her slender silhouette kneeling next to a fence post.

By the time he reached her, Adam could barely catch his breath. She knelt on the grass next to a big coil of barbed wire. He hauled her up by the shoulders and drew her into his arms. "Don't you *ever* pull a stunt like this again!"

Then he kissed her. A long, hard kiss to prove to himself she was real and alive. He pressed her body against his to reassure himself that nothing was battered or broken. But she wasn't injured. In fact, she was just right. Her alluring curves fit perfectly against him.

He gentled the kiss, letting himself enjoy the soft, yielding pressure of her mouth. She tasted sweet and safe. For one long, lingering moment, Adam didn't want to let her go.

Katie, however, didn't give him any choice. She struggled out of his embrace, a fiery blush on her cheeks. "*Me?* Me pull a stunt? You're the one who drove off and left me!"

His breathing was hard and heavy so he couldn't reply right away. He blamed it on his sprint to find her, not on the fact that their kiss had completely rocked him. "I was planning to come back," he said at last. "I wanted to teach you a lesson."

Her furious gaze fell to his mouth. "I know how to kiss, thank you very much."

He couldn't argue with that. In fact, he wanted very much to kiss her again. Especially since she seemed determined to make him feel guilty for getting her lost.

He scowled at her. "Why didn't you stay by that tree?"

"Because I didn't want to be wolf bait. Besides, how was I to know you were coming back for me? You made it perfectly clear you never wanted to see me again."

"I never said that."

She rolled her eyes. "A little cocklebur told me. Or rather, several little cockleburs. Since my pain and suffering didn't seem to bother you, why should abandoning me in the middle of nowhere!"

"I didn't dump you there on purpose," he said, truly sorry for causing her pain. He'd sit on a mountain of cockleburs if it would make her feel better. Unfortunately, he thought she might take him up on the offer. "I did say I'd help pull them out."

"You would have enjoyed it too much," she said through clenched teeth.

He couldn't help but smile at her fierce expression. "You're probably right."

"This is not funny."

His smile faded. "Neither was your harebrained idea to wander aimlessly through unfamiliar country."

"What else was I supposed to do? At least I might have stumbled across a house or a barn."

"Or into this barbed wire fence," he countered. "Or into a badger hole. Then you'd be lying out here with a broken ankle. Completely helpless." He shook his head. "I've never met such an obstinate, headstrong woman in my life."

"Is that why you kissed me?" she asked wryly.

"Do you find obstinate, headstrong women irresistible?"

"Don't worry," he said roughly, "it won't happen again."

She paled. "Oh, no."

He was surprised by her unexpected reaction. Pleasantly surprised. "I didn't really mean it. I'll kiss you again if you want me to."

"No," she cried, a look of horror suffusing her face. She turned away from him and knelt next to the fence post.

He clenched his jaw. "All right, I won't kiss you."

When she didn't react to his words, he crouched beside her. That's when he saw the small ball of fur tangled in the coil of barbed wire.

"I forgot about him," she said, her voice strained with self-recrimination and regret. "You grabbed me and kissed me and I was so surprised and...upset that I forgot all about him." As she reached out one hand, the pup tensed, its fur bristling around its neck.

Adam grabbed her wrist. "What do you think you're doing?"

"I have to get this puppy loose. He's hurt and bleeding."

"Katie, this isn't a puppy, it's a wild animal. A coyote."

"I know that," she replied, attempting to pull apart the coil of barbed wire with her free hand. Pitiful whimpers emanated from the creature's throat. She swore softly as a sharp barb punctured her thumb.

"Here, let me do it," Adam grumbled, moving

her out of the way. He bent and eased the heavy wire apart. The coyote pup growled and nipped at his hands as he tried to extricate it from the tangle of barbs and wire. Soon he couldn't tell if the blood on his hands belonged to him or the coyote. The pup gave a high-pitched yelp as Adam pulled him free.

"Don't hurt him," Katie admonished.

"He's fine," Adam assured her. "He's just terrified of people." He rose to his feet, gingerly holding the coyote pup in one outstretched hand. The pup's spindly hind legs dangled in the air. Blood from several superficial wounds matted the scraggly gray fur. The only serious wound was a deep, jagged tear in its soft white underbelly.

"The poor thing," Katie crooned, reaching out to pat its small head.

Adam pulled the pup out of her reach. "This poor thing has teeth sharp enough to bite your fingers off."

She scowled. "Adam, it's just a baby. I was feeding him the leftover barbecue before you came. Although he seemed to like the cherry pie best. He ate it right out of my hand."

Adam looked down in dismay at the empty shoe box. "You gave my barbecue and my cherry pie to a coyote?"

"He was starving," she explained. "He's hurt, too. I can't believe his mother abandoned him."

"That's the way it is in the world. Only the strong survive."

She cocked her head. "Are you always this cynical?"

"I call it realistic."

"Well, the reality is we have to take him with us."

Adam stared at her, certain he'd heard her wrong. That kiss must still be affecting him. "Would you mind repeating that?"

She tipped up her chin. "I said we're taking the coyote with us."

He nodded. "That's what I thought you said. And it's absolutely out of the question."

Her brown eyes widened in dismay. "We can't just leave him here. He'll be all alone…and afraid." She licked her lips, drawing his attention once more to her mouth. "We can at least take him back to Lightning Creek with us so the vet can have a look at him."

"We're not going back to Lightning Creek."

She blinked at him in surprise. "You're not taking me back?"

He shook his head. He'd made a promise to take her to Montana if he found her safe and sound, and he had to keep it. Adam Harper didn't make promises easily or lightly. But he always kept them. "I've decided to let you come with me to Montana."

Katie grinned as she threw her arms around his neck. "Thank you, Adam. You have no idea how much this means to me."

The pup growled deep in his chest as he found himself trapped between two human bodies. Katie laughed as she quickly moved away. "So it's finally settled. We're going to Montana."

"Without the coyote," Adam added.

"With the coyote," she insisted, planting her hands on her hips.

The next thing Adam knew they were at the car

and he was placing the injured coyote pup in the barbecue-scented shoe box. He secured the lid on top and tied it firmly with the tattered red ribbon. Katie had made several air holes in the lid, but she still didn't look happy about it.

"Why can't I just hold him in my lap?"

Adam placed the shoe box between them on the front seat. "Because he's neither tame nor potty-trained. Besides, I have to win at least one argument today or I may get cranky."

She unspooled her seat belt and latched it into place. "How will I be able to tell?"

"Very funny," he said, inserting the key into the ignition.

She reached over and squeezed his forearm. "Thank you, Adam."

"We're only taking the coyote as far as the nearest animal shelter," he reminded her.

"First we need to stop the bleeding."

Adam had already sacrificed his handkerchief, and Katie had the pup wrapped up like a mongrel mummy. "There's a small town up ahead. Maybe we can buy some gauze and bandages there."

"And buy you a new shirt," she added, wincing at the bloodstains smeared across Adam's white shirt. "I promise to make this up to you."

A wry smile tipped one corner of his mouth. "Just trying to make sure you get your forty-seven dollars and fifty-five cents worth."

He flipped on the ignition. The engine wheezed and coughed but it didn't turn over. He attempted to start it five more times, then leaned his forehead against the steering wheel and moaned in despair.

"What's wrong?" Katie asked. "Why won't the car start?"

He turned to look at her. "Because this is one of the worst days of my life."

She arched one finely winged brow. "Should I take that personally?"

"It's not you," he said with a sigh. "Lightning Creek always seems to bring me bad luck." He reached down to pop the hood. "Don't worry. The same thing happened at Lost Springs. I know how to fix it."

He climbed out of the car, lifted the hood, latched it into position, then bent down, trying to make out the various oily components in the dark. Adam wasn't a superstitious man, but he was starting to wonder if he'd ever get out of Wyoming.

After a few minutes, Katie joined him at the front bumper. "Can I help?"

Adam unscrewed the cover of the air cleaner. "Do you have a hairbrush?"

"Your hair looks fine."

"Thanks," he said dryly, "but I need something to hold this choke flap open, and the handle of a hairbrush is just about the right size."

"I've got a comb in my purse."

He carefully set the wing nut aside and lifted the cover off the air cleaner. "A comb won't work. I've got a hairbrush in my suitcase."

"Let me get it."

Adam watched her walk away, amused at her complacency now that she'd finally gotten her way. Not only did she get to go to Montana, she got to have her adopted coyote along for part of the ride.

After a few moments, he heard the hatchback slam shut, and she returned with a hairbrush in hand.

He stuck it into the choke flap, then moved to the driver's side of the car, leaning in to turn the key in the ignition.

"It works!" Katie clapped her hands as a plume of black smoke burst out of the tailpipe.

"Barely," Adam muttered. He removed the hairbrush and stuck it in his back pocket. Then he replaced the air cleaner cover and screwed it on tight. "We're not shutting it off again until we get to the airport." He slammed the hood. If he could just make it to Casper, all his troubles would be over.

"How much was the Snickers bar?" Katie asked, a pencil poised above the notepad in her lap.

"Forget it," he said, his gaze steady on the road. "The candy bar was my treat. You don't owe me anything."

Except the two hundred dollars it took to stitch up her coyote. They'd stopped at a Gas 'N Grocery in Parkerton for bandages. The store clerk's mother just happened to be a veterinarian. She'd agreed to come down and take a look at the injured coyote. Twenty stitches and two prescriptions later, they were on their way to Casper.

"The coyote is my responsibility," she insisted. "I'm the one who should pay for him." Not that she had the money to do it. A quick mental calculation told her it would take a good three months' waitressing at the Roadkill Grill to come up with the extra money.

Then it occurred to her that she'd probably never return to the Roadkill. Once she met Rodney, she'd discover everything about her past and herself. Did she have brothers and sisters? A flourishing career? A husband?

She glanced at Adam, remembering that kiss. A thrilling tingle of excitement raced through her veins when she thought of it. She'd been so relieved to see him. Then so shocked when he'd kissed her. Even more shocked at herself when she didn't want the kiss to end.

How could she possibly react that way to him if she had a husband, even if she didn't remember him? Frustrated with questions that had no answers, she focused her concentration on the ever-growing I.O.U. list. "How much do you estimate my plane ticket will cost?"

Adam flipped on the radio. The soft strains of a country ballad wafted from the back speaker. "I'm paying for your plane ticket. According to the brochure, the bachelor of your choice is supposed to provide a weekend of carefree fun." He turned to look at her, one corner of his mouth tipped up in a smile. "Are we having fun yet?"

"I am now that my ears have stopped ringing," she replied. The pup had howled and barked throughout the entire examination and treatment by the veterinarian. Both their nerves had been frayed by the experience.

"I just hope that sedative lasts until we get to the animal shelter," Adam said, glancing at the open shoe box. "Casper is just up ahead."

Casper. Katie's throat tightened as she gazed at the sleeping coyote. He looked so small and vulnerable and defenseless. Some hidden inner strength had held her together for the last two months. But now, seeing this lost, wounded pup alone in the world made her all too aware of her own fears. Her own isolation.

"Here's the plan," Adam said, unaware of her thoughts. "We'll drop the coyote off at the shelter, then head straight for the airport. We should have just enough time to buy your ticket and get on the plane."

"I can't do it," Katie said in low voice.

He frowned at her. "Don't tell me you're afraid of flying."

"No." She hesitated. "At least I don't think so."

"Then what's the problem?"

She pointed to the coyote pup sleeping so innocently in the box on her lap. "Him."

"But we already agreed to drop him at the animal shelter."

"I know. But that was before I talked to that store clerk. Do you know what they'll do with this poor, defenseless puppy?"

As if on cue, the straggly mutt opened his big dark eyes and blinked at Adam. Little did he know his days were numbered.

"I can guess," Adam muttered, then he looked away, a muscle knotting his jaw. "Katie, there's a reason for it. Coyotes are predators. They kill sheep and baby calves. They're considered a pest."

She cradled the injured pup protectively in her arms. "Well, this is one pest I'm not going to let anyone exterminate. I've got another idea."

"I'm almost certain I don't want to hear it."

She told him anyway. "Let's take him with us."

Adam almost drove off the road. "Forget it."

She tipped up her chin. "They let pets on airplanes."

He rolled his eyes. "In the first place, this is a wild animal, not a pet. In the second place, we don't have a pet carrier, and I guarantee the pilot won't let you hold a coyote on your lap during the trip. And in the third place, the airport authorities will probably take one look at him and call the animal control officers."

"Then I have another idea."

"I was afraid of that." He clenched his jaw. "What is it?"

"Let's drive to Montana."

"Drive? Do you have any idea how far we are from Butte?"

She nibbled her lower lip. "All I know is I can't leave this little guy behind. Look at him, Adam. He needs us."

Almost against his will, Adam looked at the small bundle of fur on her lap. Surely not even he could resist the pitiful sight of the small puppy covered in gauze and antibacterial ointment. "The Montana state line is several hours away. This car won't even make it that far."

She thought she heard a note of resignation in his voice. He was softening. "We can trade it in for another one at the rental company. It's already after midnight, so traffic will be light. We'll be in Butte before you know it."

A Welcome To Casper sign loomed in the distance. She held her breath, waiting for him to make a final decision.

At last he released a haggard sigh. "According to the bachelor auction rules you get to choose how to spend the weekend. If you want to spend it driving all the way to Montana, then we'll drive all the way to Montana.''

Once they reached Casper, they traded in the lemon for a red four-wheel drive. Katie transferred the sleeping coyote and Adam's suitcase into the new vehicle while Adam took care of the paperwork inside the rental office. Twenty minutes later, they were on the way, heading north on Interstate 25.

Butte, Montana, lay only five hundred miles away.

CHAPTER FOUR

"KATIE."

Adam's husky voice floated over her like a caress. His hands smoothed her hair, sending little tingles of pleasure through her. He leaned closer, making her heart beat faster as his lips skimmed her hair. "I'm yours," he whispered. "All yours."

She moaned as his lips trailed a sensuous path down her neck, his hands curling around her shoulders. Then he shook her.

"Katie, wake up!"

She jerked awake, her knee hitting the dashboard. She blinked twice to clear her vision, then turned to look at Adam. He removed his hand from her shoulder as he shifted behind the steering wheel.

It had been a dream. Just a dream. She took a deep breath, her heart still racing. If Adam Harper could do that to her in a dream, she didn't want to think about the effect he could have on her awake.

"I must have dozed off for a minute," she said, rubbing her knee.

"You've been asleep for the last two hours."

Katie looked out the window and realized they weren't moving. "Where are we?"

"The Valentine Motel. I think we'll both be more comfortable in a nice, soft bed."

She swallowed as the images from her dream

came rushing back. *Comfortable* wasn't exactly the word she'd use to describe the two of them sharing a bed. Hot. Erotic. Impossible. Not that she wasn't tempted. Her stomach fluttered every time she looked into his sky blue eyes. But she'd met him less than twenty-four hours ago.

And she wore a wedding ring on her finger.

He climbed out of the car and tossed her the keys. "Why don't you get the luggage out of the back while I go register." Then he was gone.

Katie slowly got out of the car. The motel sat on a deserted strip of highway, the white paint peeling on the short row of numbered doors. A red neon vacancy sign flashed in the office window. She moved around the back of the car, unlocked the hatchback and popped it open. A brisk north wind sent a shiver down her spine. Or maybe it was the sight of Adam walking toward her, a room key in his hand.

"I left a wake-up call for eight o'clock," he said. "That should get us to Montana in plenty of time." He reached inside the car and grabbed his suitcase.

Katie cleared her throat. "Adam, there's something you should know."

He turned to her. "About your suitcase?"

She blinked at him in surprise. "What?"

"Where's your suitcase?"

"I didn't have time to pack one."

He closed the hatchback, his face grim. "So you don't have anything except the clothes on your back?"

"I have the coyote."

"Thanks for reminding me," he said dryly, then reached inside the car and grabbed the shoe box.

"All right, let's go. Maybe things will look better in the morning."

She trailed behind him as he walked briskly toward the motel. He stopped in front of room seven and inserted the key in the lock. Then he walked inside, leaving the door open behind him.

Katie took a deep breath as she stood in the open doorway. A double bed occupied the center of the room, flanked on either side by a small nightstand. A pair of moss-green chintz drapes covered the window, matching the nubby green carpet on the floor.

What would he do when she refused to sleep with him? Lose his temper? Kick her out of the room? Leave her behind tomorrow morning? She didn't even want to think about that possibility. Instead, she had to find a way to let him down gently. To cushion the blow that he'd be sleeping alone tonight.

She squared her shoulders and stepped inside the motel room. Adam had placed the shoe box under the window and was draping a spare blanket over the sleeping pup. He looked up when she shut the door behind her, placing a finger over his lips. "He's starting to stir a little."

She glanced at the coyote, then motioned for Adam to follow her into the bathroom. She flipped on the light, illuminating the chipped white tile on the walls and the dinky bathtub.

"We have to talk," she said, after Adam had closed the bathroom door behind him.

"It's after midnight," he replied in the same husky tones he'd used in her dream. "Can't we talk in the morning?"

"This can't wait."

He folded his arms and leaned against the door.

The bathroom suddenly seemed much smaller with him in it. And warmer.

"Did the puppy go back to sleep?" she asked, stalling for time. Adam looked rumpled and tired and gorgeous, and she had to remind herself of all the reasons sharing a bed with him was not a good idea.

"It's a coyote," he reminded her. "And, yes, he's asleep."

She nodded. "We really have to come up with a name for him. We can't just keep calling him the coyote."

"We're not going to keep him. He's a wild animal, not a pet." Then his brow furrowed. "Is this what you wanted to talk about—naming the coyote?"

"Actually, I wanted to talk about the sleeping arrangements."

He quirked an eyebrow. "What about them?"

"Well...I have a bad back," she improvised. "And these soft motel mattresses are the worst."

"This bed is hard as a rock. I tried it out."

"I still prefer to sleep...in the bathtub."

"The *bathtub?*"

She forced a smile. "I'm sure with a pillow and a blanket it will be nice and cozy."

He frowned at the compact tub. "You'll have to sleep with your feet hanging over the edge."

"It's better than the alternative," she muttered. At least she'd be so uncomfortable she wouldn't have any more erotic dreams.

"What alternative?"

"A sore back in the morning."

"I see." He sighed, rubbing one hand over the

rough whiskers on his jaw. "I wish you would have told me this sooner. I could have saved money on that other motel room."

"Other motel room?" she echoed.

He pulled a key from his pocket and held it up. "I've got room eight, right next to yours. If I'd known you sleep in bathtubs we could have shared a room and saved thirty bucks."

Two rooms? She didn't know whether to be embarrassed or insulted. Shouldn't he at least *want* to sleep with her? Obviously the thought had never crossed his mind.

"Do you want me to tuck you into the bathtub before I go?" he asked, a smile playing on his lips.

"No, thank you," she said, her face warm. She had the uncomfortable feeling he knew she'd been lying through her teeth about her bad back. "I can manage on my own."

He bid her good night, then walked out of the bathroom. She waited several minutes before peeking out the door. He was gone. With a sigh of relief, she stripped off her clothes, washed her underthings in the sink and hung them on the towel rack to drip-dry.

Then she walked to the big, empty bed and slid between the starched cotton sheets. Adam was right about the mattress, it was rock hard. She didn't have a bad back now, but chances were good she'd develop one by morning.

It had been an exhausting day, both physically and mentally, but sleep eluded her. Nights were always the worst for Katie. The time she felt the most alone. And the most vulnerable. The time she remembered that someone had deliberately caused her car accident. Her vivid imagination took flight, and the shadows around her became ominous.

Katie pulled the blanket over her head. "This is ridiculous, Katie Scarlett O'Hara," she muttered to herself, but she stayed under the blanket. At long last, the warmth of the bedclothes relaxed her and she fell into a deep, uneasy sleep.

ADAM PULLED the pillow over his head. *Sleep.* That's all he wanted, a few hours of uninterrupted sleep. Unfortunately, there was a coyote in the next room. A noisy coyote. He'd barely drifted off when the sound of claws scratching against the wall had awakened him. Then came a long, keening howl. How could one puny coyote make so much racket?

And why didn't Katie do something about it?

"Because an earthquake wouldn't wake her up," he muttered, remembering how long it had taken him to awaken her in the car. How tempted he'd been to wake her with a kiss, just like Sleeping Beauty. But a man didn't take advantage of an unconscious woman. No matter how enticing her lips had looked in the moonlight.

He closed his eyes, remembering the sweep of her long auburn eyelashes against her creamy cheeks. The soft purr in her throat when he'd brushed back her hair. The satiny smoothness of her skin when he'd wiggled her shoulder.

"Arrrooooo!"

His eyes snapped open at the plaintive howl. "Damn. This is ridiculous." Adam sat up in bed. Thinking about kissing Katie wasn't helping him fall asleep. Just the opposite. He pulled on his denim jeans as he heard the coyote subside into a series of frantic yips. Then he stomped out the door.

He pounded on Katie's door, but she didn't open it. "The bathroom must be soundproof," he muttered, pulling his pocket knife out of his jeans. A few deft twists and turns with the thin blade of the knife, and the lock emitted a satisfying click. He was in. And the coyote was in big trouble.

The room was dark, but he could just make out a slender form under the blanket on the bed. *Katie.* She must have decided to take her chances with the mattress. A smile quirked up his lips. Maybe the bed seemed less risky now that she knew he wasn't in it. Adam knew he should have told her about the separate rooms right away, but he'd been having too much fun watching her squirm.

His smile faded as his gaze fell on the coyote pup gnawing on the drapes. "Hey," he muttered. "Cut that out."

The pup's ears pricked up at the sound. Or maybe it had picked up his scent and sensed danger was near, because Adam was ready to wring its scrawny little neck. The pup turned its attention from the drapes to Adam. A low growl emanated from its throat that ruffled the fur around its neck.

"Cut the tough guy act," Adam whispered.

The coyote cocked his head as Adam stalked toward him. Then the pup quickly scampered to the shoe box, lying down with his chin tucked between his paws.

"Don't play innocent with me," Adam muttered, grabbing the box and hauling it into the bathroom. "You're nothing but a furry ball of trouble."

As Adam placed the box in the bathtub, the pup

sat up and licked his hand. "It's too late to play nice now. If I had my way, you'd be outside with all the other varmints."

Adam had to admit this varmint had a certain rascally charm about him. The pup lapped his tongue over Adam's knuckles, then began chasing his own straggly tail.

"I see you're feeling better," Adam remarked, reaching for the prescription bottle of sedatives on the bathroom sink. The veterinarian had warned them to keep the pup sedated for at least twelve hours to prevent him from tearing out his stitches.

"Here you go." He held out his hand, and the pup nibbled the pill from his palm. "That's a good boy," Adam said, kneeling to pat his furry head.

The pup lapped at his palm, looking for another pill. Finding it empty, he turned his attention elsewhere. Before Adam could stop him, the pup lunged at something white, lacy and wet hanging from the towel rack.

"You're too young to play with that," he muttered as the pup furiously wiggled his head back and forth, snapping the dainty bra in the air. Adam latched onto a slim strap, but the pup wouldn't let go. They engaged in a tug-of-war, the pup growling low in his throat as Adam tried to wrestle the bra free.

"Let go," Adam ordered, getting a firmer grip on the delicate scrap of silk and lace. To his surprise, the pup obeyed. Then it jumped into its box, circled once and lay down.

Adam stood, holding Katie's bra in his hands. He couldn't very well leave it in here for the pup to tear to pieces. Or the lacy pair of panties still hanging on the rack.

When the pup finally drifted to sleep, Adam crept out of the bathroom, holding Katie's bra in one hand and her panties in the other. He glanced at the still form under the blanket. If she woke up right now, this wouldn't look too good. He quickly draped the bra and panties on the rabbit ears of the television antenna, then moved toward the door.

He hesitated, his hand on the doorknob. Lingerie hanging from the television antenna might look a little strange to her. No doubt she'd wonder how it got there. He should probably tell her he'd sedated the coyote again, too. He didn't want the little guy suffering from an accidental overdose.

How had he ever gotten into this situation? He was in a cheap motel room with a woman he'd only met a few hours ago and her pet coyote. He rubbed one hand over the rough whiskers on his jaw, then moved into the room, aware of Katie's soft, somnolent breathing. He'd never met anyone like her before, and if he was lucky, he never would again. Adam didn't like complications, and Katie O'Hara was definitely a complication. She was also keeping something from him. No woman would go to all the trouble she did just for a weekend with him. He was modest enough to know he wasn't that great a catch. So why the desperate measures to get to Montana?

Adam crept to the side of the bed and carefully pulled the blanket off her face. Her silky auburn curls spilled across the white pillowcase. She looked deceptively innocent, but he knew from recent experience that she could wreak havoc in his life.

"Katie?" He kneeled beside the bed, then

reached out one hand to shake her awake, his fingertips skimming over the warm, bare skin beneath her collarbone. That's when he realized she probably didn't have any clothes on under the blanket. Before he could react to that disconcerting fact, Katie's eyes drifted open. She blinked once.

Then she screamed.

STILL CAUGHT on the fringes of her nightmare, Katie was only aware of a big, half-naked man hovering over her bed. Guided by an instinct of self-preservation and a surge of adrenaline, she grabbed the telephone and hurled it at his head. It caught him on the temple, and he emitted a surprised grunt of pain.

Katie's heart raced as she scrambled to the other side of the bed. She hit the floor running, the polyester bedspread clutched to her chest.

"Are you trying to kill me?" A familiar voice barked the words as she reached the door.

"Adam?" Katie turned, trying to make out the man's features in the darkness. Then she reached out and flipped on the overheard light.

Adam sat on the edge of the bed holding one side of his head. Blood trickled between his fingers and dripped onto his bare chest.

"Oh, no!" Katie hurried to his side. "Are you all right?"

"I'm barely conscious," he replied, his face pale. "What did you think you were doing?"

"What was I doing?" she exclaimed, wrapping the bedspread around her like a toga. "What are you doing in my room in the middle of the night? I thought you were...." Her voice trailed off as she clasped her trembling fingers together.

Adam closed his eyes and groaned softly as he held his head in his hands. "I came to muzzle your furry little friend. I couldn't sleep with his constant howling."

"I didn't hear anything." She looked around the room. "Where is he? What have you done with my coyote?"

"He's curled up in the bathtub, sound asleep. I figured he could do less damage in there if he woke up again. I just wanted to tell you I'd given him another sedative."

But Katie wasn't paying any attention to him. She was staring at the television antenna. Her panties and bra hung suspended on the aluminum tips, dripping onto the carpet.

Adam cleared his throat. "I can explain."

She took a step away from him, not certain she wanted an explanation for something this bizarre. "Maybe you should just go back to your room."

"Not until you let me explain," he insisted. "The puppy wanted to play tug-of-war with your bra, and I won. But coyotes are sneaky, so I knew I couldn't leave your lingerie in the bathroom."

"So you put it on the antenna?"

He nodded, wincing at the motion. "For safe-keeping."

"Thanks...I guess."

"Don't mention it." He closed his eyes and leaned back on the bed. "Now, if you don't mind, I'm going to bleed to death in your bed. The car keys are on the dresser in my room. Have a good time in Montana."

She bit back a smile. Now that her terror had faded, she could almost feel sorry for him. "Don't you think you might be overreacting just a little bit?"

He slanted one eye open. "Overreacting? I probably have a concussion."

"I didn't hit you that hard."

"I'm bleeding," he whined. "I'll probably need stitches."

"Let me see," she said, pulling his hand away from the wound.

"Ow!"

She breathed a sigh of relief. "It's only a tiny cut. I can hardly see it."

"Well, I definitely feel it."

"Just rest here a moment," Katie said, before slipping into the bathroom, where she exchanged the bedspread for her denim dress. After soaking a washcloth with warm water, she returned to Adam's side, the bedsprings squeaking as she sat on the edge of the mattress.

He opened his eyes as she began dabbing at the cut on his head. "That hurts."

"Do you want me to kiss it and make it all better?" she teased.

He frowned. "I'm glad you find my pain and suffering so amusing."

"I'm sorry," she murmured, gently wiping the blood from his chest. "If I'd known it was you, I probably never would have hit you with the telephone."

"Probably?"

"Well, it would depend on your intentions," she murmured, gently stroking her fingers through his hair. "After all, you did break into my room half naked. What's a girl to think?"

"For your information, I don't need to attack unwilling women in their hotel rooms." His eyelids drifted shut as she kept up the soothing strokes. "I've never had trouble finding female companionship."

She didn't doubt it for a moment. Not when she had proof of his appeal right before her eyes. Like the taut, finely honed muscles of his chest. His ruggedly handsome face. His whiskey-smooth voice.

Even now, as he relaxed into a deep, peaceful sleep, she couldn't stop touching him. Her fingertips stroked his forehead and across the rough whiskers on his cheek. She traced the curve of his ear and trailed her fingers down the column of his neck to his broad shoulders.

When her fingers reached the dark, silky hairs on his chest, she drew back, appalled at her actions. Was she nuts? She barely knew this man. And she definitely didn't want to know him any better. Not when she might have another man waiting for her somewhere.

Katie abruptly stood up, her knees wobbly. She had to stick to her plan. She couldn't let a wounded coyote or an incredibly handsome man distract her. In a few short hours she'd meet Rodney Tate.

Then all her problems would be solved.

CHAPTER FIVE

KATIE SLOWLY AWOKE from a deep, dreamless sleep, trying desperately to ignore the annoying tickling sensation under her nose. She kept her eyes firmly closed, burrowing her cheek into the soft, warm, hairy pillow.

Hairy? Her eyes shot open, and she found herself curled up on the bed next to Adam, her head resting on his chest. She could hear the steady beat of his heart and feel his arms wrapped around her. Even worse, her hand lay splayed over his navel, her fingertips hidden beneath the waistband of his jeans. With a gasp of horror, she sat straight up in bed, her cheeks burning.

"Morning, sleepyhead," Adam said, his voice low and husky. "How's your back?"

"My back? It's fine.... I mean, it's really sore." She placed her hand on her lower back, faking a grimace as she stretched. She didn't know how long she could carry on this bad-back charade. She certainly didn't want to spend the rest of the weekend sleeping in a bathtub.

Adam clasped his hands behind his head as he leaned back against the pillows. "Well, I appreciate the sacrifice."

"Sacrifice?" she echoed, confused.

"Watching over me on this horrible mattress

when you could have gotten a good night's sleep in the bathtub.'' Then he grinned.

"All right, I confess. I don't have a bad back.''

"No kidding," he said wryly. "Anyone with a bad back could not have contorted herself into a pretzel to fit in the hatchback of that rental car.''

Katie twisted the ring on her finger. "It's nothing personal, I just didn't want to sleep with you last night. But I didn't know how to tell you without hurting your feelings.''

"I've got a thick skin," he replied. "And, Katie?''

"Yes?''

"You did sleep with me last night.''

He didn't need to remind her. She was all too aware of the way she'd nestled up against him during the night. She'd only meant to rest her eyes for a moment. She'd been worried about the bump on his head, which had blossomed into an impressive blue and purple knot. It would look great in the wedding pictures.

"Any regrets?''

Only the fact that she couldn't take her eyes off him. The white cotton sheet slid down to his waist, exposing all of his broad chest and washboard stomach. She swallowed, her mouth suddenly dry. She needed to remember her priorities. She needed a cold shower.

"I'll...go wash up," she said, practically running to the bathroom. When she emerged twenty minutes later, she found Adam up and dressed and sitting on the edge of the bed.

"I've come up with the perfect name for your coyote.''

"What?" she asked, towel-drying her hair.

"How do you like the name Wile E. Coyote?"

She turned toward the television just in time to see the hapless cartoon coyote plunge off a cliff. He did look a little like her coyote, especially with the limp and the bandages. "All right, we'll call him Wiley for short."

"This is one of my favorites." Adam nodded toward the television. "Wile E. shoots himself out of a cannon."

One of his favorites? She bit back a smile as she realized her tough bachelor liked cartoons. A sexy man on the outside and a little boy on the inside. Who could possibly resist that combination?

"I can," she muttered under her breath, determined to keep her mind focused today.

He turned to her. "Did you say something?"

She cleared her throat. "I said I can hardly wait to get to Montana. Are you about ready?"

"Oh...sure." With an air of reluctance, Adam aimed the remote at the television set and pressed the power button off. "At least today we don't have to worry about car trouble."

It took them an hour and a pair of jumper cables to get the four-wheel drive started. Then they had to stop for doughnuts for Adam and puppy chow for Wiley. By noon they'd reached the Montana state line. By one o'clock they arrived in Butte, where they traded their car for a Chevy Blazer at the rental company.

"This is more like it," Adam said as he cruised the Blazer into a department-store parking lot.

"What are we doing here?" Katie asked, petting the head of the sedated coyote in her lap.

"Buying you some necessities, like clothes."

She set the sleeping pup in the shoe box. "I can't let you spend any more money on me."

"Well, I'm afraid you don't have a choice," Adam said, popping open his door. "Rodney gets perfect reception on his satellite dish, so you won't be able to dry your lingerie on the television antenna."

Katie soon found out he had more than lingerie on his mind. Ignoring her protests, he purchased her two sets of clothes, a nightgown, makeup, perfume and an expensive pair of leather hiking boots. She spent the remainder of the trip tallying up the additional costs on her I.O.U. list and wondering if he'd let her repay him on an installment plan.

"This is it," Adam announced as he parked in front of the security gate bordering the Tate estate.

Katie stared in awe at the mansion behind the gate. It was a sprawling redbrick colonial with four round white pillars flanking the front entrance. In the middle of the circular drive was a three-tiered fountain. Tate's place was big and intimidating and not at all what she'd imagined.

Hit with a sudden attack of nerves, she dropped the pencil in her hand. How would Rodney Tate react when he saw her? Would he be happy? Surprised? Disappointed? She couldn't help but remember Sheriff Hatcher's troubled eyes when he explained that her car accident looked suspicious. Both of her back tires had been shot out as she rounded a curve on Shoshone Highway. One blown tire might be explained away by a hunter's stray bullet. But two?

Was that why she didn't want to remember? Was

there something, or more likely, *someone* in her past who wanted her dead? Could that someone possibly be Rodney Tate?

She saw Adam reach for the gearshift. "Wait!" she exclaimed, grabbing his arm.

He turned to her. "What's wrong?"

"Tell me about Rodney Tate." Her heart pounded in her chest, and Katie couldn't seem to catch her breath.

He stared at her a moment, his dark brow furrowed. "What exactly do you want to know?"

"Everything."

ADAM WAS USED to heavy breathing during his dates, but no woman had ever hyperventilated before. At least Katie hadn't passed out. Her cheeks regained some of their color as she slowly breathed in and out of the paper bag.

"Better?" he asked, after she lowered the bag to her lap.

"Yes, I'm fine now." She emitted a shaky laugh as she tucked a stray curl behind one ear. "Guess I'm a little nervous about meeting your friend."

Funny how she wasn't nervous about stowing away in the car of a perfect stranger. Or adopting a wild coyote. Or assaulting him with a telephone. So why should she suddenly be apprehensive about meeting Rodney?

"There's no reason to be nervous," Adam replied, leaning against the driver's seat. "Rodney is just a regular guy."

She looked at the house. "He must be loaded."

Not only loaded, but a prime target for ambitious gold diggers. No doubt a waitress from Lightning

Springs would be impressed by Rodney's obvious
wealth. His parents had left him a hefty trust fund,
made available to him on his twenty-fifth birthday.
Last year Rodney had appeared in a national magazine as one of the country's most eligible bachelors.

He glanced at Katie, suspicion churning in his
gut. Strange how she'd known all about Rodney's
upcoming nuptials. And how incredibly determined
she'd been to accompany Adam to his wedding.
Now she wanted to know everything about Tate.

She was still staring at the house. "Why does he
live out here in the middle of nowhere? Isn't his
business located in Chicago?"

Rodney's business? Then he realized that Katie
didn't know Adam owned half of it. And what she
didn't know wouldn't hurt her. Or him. "The corporate headquarters are located in Chicago, but Rodney does most of the software development out here.
He thinks there is less chance of piracy in an isolated
spot."

She looked around the rugged landscape. "I think
most of the pirates would get lost just trying to find
the place."

He bit back a smile. She might be a gold digger,
but she was a charming gold digger. And what if he
was wrong? What if she didn't have any ulterior
motives? He'd been cynical about women for so
long, it was hard to imagine that possibility. He
rubbed the knot on his forehead, wondering if she'd
knocked something loose up there. He'd never been
this confused about a woman before.

But why else would she go to all this trouble to
come with him to Montana? She'd known he was

headed to Tate's place before she'd bought him. It was probably the *reason* she'd bought him. And why she and her friend had spread that impotency rumor, just to make certain no one else would want him.

"So Rodney is a cautious businessman," Katie said, breaking into his reverie.

"It's necessary in this business." He nodded toward the house. "Even clear out here. We have to run background checks on his employees and household staff. Even Rodney's girlfriends."

She paled. "So what happens to one of his girlfriends if she doesn't pass the background check?"

His hand tightened on the steering wheel. "Why? Are you thinking of applying for the position?"

She blinked at him. "Of course not. I'm just...curious."

Adam shrugged. "Actually, it's never gotten that far. His girlfriends usually dump him before the background check is complete." He'd been surprised Tate's engagement had lasted this long and was more than a little curious to meet his fiancée.

Katie didn't say anything, she just stared at the house as she twisted the ring on her finger. Maybe she was having second thoughts. Maybe Tate didn't seem like such a good catch after all. Especially since he was engaged to be married in three days.

"Any more questions?" Adam asked.

She took a deep breath. "No. I think I'm ready." Then she turned to him, her hand on his forearm. "If I don't get a chance to tell you, Adam, I just want to thank you for...everything. I'll never forget you."

That was a kiss-off speech if he ever heard one.

"Glad I could be of service." He clenched his jaw as he rolled down the car window and punched the code into the security panel. Could she possibly think Tate would dump his fiancée for a perfect stranger? Then again, look how Katie had turned Adam inside-out with little more than a kiss.

If she wanted Rodney, the poor guy didn't stand a chance.

KATIE TOOK SLOW, deep breaths, trying not to hyperventilate again as they stood at the front door. This was it. No more delays. No more wild speculation. She was about to discover her past. Her name. Her life. Rodney Tate held the key, and she could hardly wait to see what lay behind the door.

A giddiness rose inside her. She might soon be reunited with brothers and sisters she didn't know she had. A mother and father. Maybe even sons and daughters. And, more than likely, a husband.

Would he be anything like the man standing beside her? Sexy? Strong? A barbecue sauce aficionado? Katie mentally shook herself. No more guessing games, she told herself firmly. They only frustrated her, and she needed all her wits about her to pull off this meeting. She turned to Adam, surprised to see him staring at her.

"For the third time," he said slowly, "are you ready to go in?"

"I think so," she replied, her heart hammering in her chest. *Ready or not, Rodney Tate, here I come.*

Adam swiftly punched in a long series of numbers on the security keypad next to the door.

"You know all the codes to his security system?" Katie asked, surprised.

"I designed it." A bell sounded somewhere inside and the door clicked open. "After you," Adam said, holding the door open for her.

Katie walked slowly through the door, marveling at the polished black marble floor of the entryway. She turned slowly, wondering if she'd ever been here before. "Who designed this place?"

"Rodney. It's a replica of the house he grew up in."

She looked at the high cathedral ceiling. "Looks like a great place to hold a wedding."

A wry smile tipped one corner of his mouth. "If there is a wedding. Rodney's been engaged four times."

"*Four* times?" Katie couldn't help but wonder if she was one of his discards. Is that why she remembered him? Did he dump her at the altar? Or maybe *she* dumped *him*. Maybe he'd wanted revenge and shot out her tires.

"Try not to mention it," Adam said as he guided her through the entryway into a spacious sunroom. "Tate doesn't have good luck with women, and he's a little sensitive about it."

Katie nodded as she looked around the cheery room. The white wicker furniture was upholstered with blue gingham fabric. The same fabric adorned the row of matching French doors that led to a formal garden. But what caught her attention was the arrangement of photographs in rattan frames completely covering one wall.

In the center of the grouping was an eight-by-ten color photograph of Rodney Tate. The same picture she'd seen in the bachelor auction brochure. Recognition welled inside her once more. *She knew this man*. But how? Capturing the memory eluded her, like trying to hold a soap bubble before it popped.

"Look familiar?" Adam asked, standing beside her.

Katie jumped. "Why do you ask?"

He shrugged. "Just wondering. You can't seem to take your eyes off him."

She twisted the ring on her finger. "Actually, he does look a little familiar. I wonder if I've met him somewhere before."

"I doubt it," Adam replied. "Rodney doesn't get out much. And as far as I know, he hasn't been back to Lightning Creek in years."

She nodded as another photograph caught her eye. It was a faded picture of two boys, younger versions of Adam and Rodney. She could just make out the Lost Springs bunkhouse in the background. Each boy stood by a horse, though Adam held both pairs of reins in his hands. She couldn't stop staring at his eyes. That same sky blue, but in a younger, achingly boyish face. Katie sighed. No wonder so many girls had broken their hearts over him.

Rodney, standing pale and thin next to him, looked terrified. For some reason, the pair reminded her of Batman and an anemic Robin. "Tell me about this picture."

"There's nothing to tell." He folded his arms. "At Lost Springs we each had our own horse and had to feed and groom and care for it. It was supposed to teach us responsibility."

"Rodney doesn't look too happy about it."

Adam chuckled. "He's always hated horses."

She glanced at him. "So you did his work for him?"

He shrugged. "Somebody had to take care of the kid."

On the heels of that remark, Rodney Tate burst into the room.

"Hey, Harper, you made it!" Rodney reached out to shake Adam's hand, then his gaze fell on the swollen black-and-blue knot distorting his forehead. "Man, what happened to you?"

"A crank call."

Rodney grinned. "Do you want to explain that one?"

Adam glanced at Katie. "Not really."

At last, Rodney turned to her. She held her breath, waiting for that spark of recognition in his myopic green eyes. He stared at her. His jaw dropped open. Then he took a step toward her and held out his hand. "I don't believe it."

Katie clasped her hand in his, hoping he wouldn't notice how much her fingers were trembling. He gently squeezed her hand as his gaze slowly traveled from her head to her toes and back again, obviously savoring every inch of her.

"This is quite a surprise," he said at last.

"A pleasant one...I hope," she stammered.

He grinned. "The best." Then he looked at Adam. "She's the stripper, right? For my bachelor party."

Katie's jaw dropped. *Stripper?* Is that how she knew him, from some strip joint runway?

"She's not a stripper," Adam said evenly.

"Bummer."

Katie's heart dropped to her toes at the same time she let go of his hand. He didn't recognize her. He didn't *know* her. She'd done everything...bought

Adam at the auction, stowed away in his car, traveled all those endlessly long miles...for nothing. Her throat constricted painfully, and for one brief moment she couldn't breathe.

Adam's arm curled around her waist. "This is Katie O'Hara. And she's with me." As he drew her close to him, Katie's tension eased just a little. Adam stood tall and strong beside her, his warm body giving her comfort. She inhaled a long, deep breath, then another, telling herself to calm down.

Rodney pushed his wire-rim glasses up on his nose. "Since when did you let any woman get her hooks into you?"

"It's not like that," Katie heard herself say, her mind still reeling from the disappointment. She made a conscious effort to pay attention to the conversation. "I bought Adam at the Lost Springs bachelor auction."

Rodney's eyes widened. "The bachelor auction? Really?"

Adam's arm tightened around her. "You missed some great barbecue."

"That's obviously not all I missed." Rodney's gaze traversed her once again.

She swallowed. "Adam graciously agreed to bring me to Montana with him." She ignored the stifled snort beside her. "I hope you don't mind, Mr. Tate."

Rodney took a step closer to her. "I'll only mind if you keep calling me Mr. Tate." He smiled. "Call me Rodney, and I'll call you..."

"Miss O'Hara," Adam suggested.

"Katie," Rodney said instead, then ushered her

to a chair. "Can I get you some wine, or perhaps a glass of lemonade?"

"No, thank you," she replied, her stomach still in knots.

Rodney turned to Adam. "So how was your trip?"

Adam sat on the love seat. "Eventful. We picked up a…puppy along the way. I had your foreman make up a stall for him in the stables."

Katie blinked in surprise. "Stables? But I thought Mr. Tate hated horses."

"Rodney," he reminded her with a smile. "So I see Adam's told you all my secrets."

"For her own protection," Adam quipped.

Rodney laughed. "Well, we've got quite a celebration going on here for the next few days. I never realized there was so much to planning a wedding."

"Where are you holding the ceremony?" Katie asked politely, amazed at the icy calm that had overtaken her. She hadn't even considered the fact that Rodney might not recognize her.

"In the garden," Rodney replied. "It was Darla's idea. She's my fiancée." He glanced at his watch. "Darla had to drive to Butte to pick up some decorations for the wedding, but she should be back in time for the party." He grinned. "Of course, it goes without saying that you're both invited."

Adam arched a brow. "Party?"

"A cocktail party. Call it a prewedding celebration. Formal attire, of course." Rodney stood up. "I'm sure you both must be tired after your trip. Let me show you to your room."

"Rooms," Adam clarified, extending his hand to Katie.

Rodney looked surprised. "Rooms it is, then."

As they walked toward the door, Katie glanced over her shoulder for one last look at the eight-by-ten of Rodney Tate. It still set off a buzzer in her head. She knew him. So why didn't he recognize her? *Or did he?*

Somehow…some way, she had to find out.

AN HOUR LATER, Adam sat with Rodney in the library, sharing a drink before dinner. Adam didn't like this room any better than the others in the house. It was tastefully decorated, with only the most expensive artwork and furnishings, but it didn't have any depth. Sometimes he wondered the same thing about the man seated opposite him.

"Stay away from her," Adam warned as he stared at the dark amber whiskey in his glass. "You're an engaged man, remember?"

Rodney sighed. "Sometimes I wish I could forget. Marriage is a big step."

"Don't tell me you're getting cold feet."

"More like lukewarm. Darla really is wonderful. I can't wait for you to meet her." Rodney swirled the whiskey in his glass. "Of course, then I see a woman like Katie and I wonder if I'm really ready to settle down."

He knew it. He'd seen that look in Rodney's eyes before. Adam swallowed a sip of whiskey, letting the fiery liquid burn down his throat. Typical Tate, wanting something he couldn't have. Growing up at Lost Springs, he'd always wanted the best bed, the best horse, the best car. He'd wanted Adam for his friend because he was the best fighter. It never seemed to occur to Rodney that his selfishness alienated people. Or else he just didn't know any better.

Rodney's parents had made him believe he was the center of the universe. Unfortunately, when he'd arrived at Lost Springs, he hadn't understood why nobody else shared that opinion. Adam couldn't relate, especially when his mother had tossed him out like yesterday's garbage. But he'd still looked out for the kid.

Despite all the problems Rodney had caused him, Adam had always thought of him as the little brother he'd never had. An irritating, bothersome little brother who still occasionally needed some sense knocked into him.

"There's been a breach of security at the Chicago office."

Rodney's eyes widened at the sudden change of subject. "Exactly what kind of breach?"

"Some woman got into the personnel files and has been snooping around in other places, too."

Rodney frowned. "When did this happen?"

"About two months ago."

"Two *months* ago? Why the hell am I just finding out about it now?"

"Because you couldn't do anything from Montana except worry," Adam explained calmly. "And we both know when you worry you don't get any work done. Besides, I'm head of security and I'm handling it."

"So who is she?"

Adam shrugged. "That's what I want to know. Unfortunately, she didn't leave her name or any fingerprints behind." He took a sip of his whiskey. "I've reprogrammed all the security codes, but she's still out there somewhere."

Rodney threw up his hands. "What if she comes here? I've got a houseful of wedding guests with more on the way. What if she's one of them?"

"Don't you know who you invited?"

"Of course. But there's always people you don't know at a wedding. I'd probably assume this woman was a friend of Darla's, and Darla would assume she's a friend of mine."

"I already checked out all the guests on the invitation list you sent me three weeks ago. None of them match her description. But you're right, we'll still have to keep our eyes open."

"So what exactly does she look like?" Rodney asked.

"A leggy redhead."

Rodney stared at him. "That's it? That's all we've got to go on?"

"My doorman doesn't pay a lot of attention to details. He did say she was sexy."

Rodney rolled his eyes. "Well, that really narrows it down. She could be anybody. Hell, your girlfriend fits that description."

The hairs prickled on the back of Adam's neck. "She's not my girlfriend."

"But she is sexy," Rodney countered. "And a redhead. Makes me almost wish I'd gone on the auction block myself instead of sending you in my place."

"That makes two of us." The humiliation of that moment washed over him once again, and he drained his shot glass.

"The money went to a good cause," Rodney reminded him.

"I'd already made a donation," he said between clenched teeth. "You could have done the same."

"You know I don't like to throw my money around. Besides, why are you complaining? You ended up with one hell of a woman. If she'd bought me—"

"She didn't."

"Well, I'm not so sure about that," Rodney said with a grin. "Technically, you were just substituting for me. So she bought me by proxy, if you will."

"The hell she did."

Rodney chuckled. "Hey, I'm just joking around. Why would I want any other woman when I've got Darla? She is really something, Adam. Even better than that cheerleader you dated in college, remember her?"

"Not really."

Rodney looked at him in amazement. "I don't believe it. You *have* to remember her. Her name was Rhonda and she had the best breasts on campus. She was really heartbroken when you broke up with her." He grinned. "Fortunately, I was there to pick up the pieces."

Adam laughed. "You were always good at that."

"I've repaired so many broken hearts I could be a cardiologist. Too bad I'll have to give up my practice after the wedding."

"I don't suppose your wife would understand."

"Definitely not." Rodney smiled. "Darla is the jealous type. She doesn't like any other woman taking my attention away from her."

"Sounds like you picked the right one this time."

"Maybe," Rodney said thoughtfully as he stared at the ceiling. "Maybe."

CHAPTER SIX

KATIE PACED back and forth across her upstairs bedroom. It was more like a lavish suite. Rodney Tate definitely knew how to make his guests comfortable. The finest ivory silk and lace fabrics spilled from the windows and upholstered the chaise longue and overstuffed chairs. A beautiful lace coverlet that could only be handmade covered the queen-size bed, accented with coral and ivory striped pillows, and fine coral gauze was draped from the overhead canopy.

But all the froth and lace didn't distract her from her most immediate problem. Rodney didn't know her. And now Katie didn't know what to do. She hadn't even planned for that possibility.

She must know him, or his picture wouldn't have looked so familiar to her. A cold dread trickled through her veins as she realized his picture looked more familiar to her than the man himself. Maybe she'd seen him in a newspaper or magazine photo sometime in the past. Or maybe that strong sense of recognition was just a figment of her imagination. She didn't want to consider that possibility. It meant she couldn't trust her own judgment or instincts.

"Get a grip, O'Hara," she told herself firmly, swallowing the lump in her throat. She *wasn't* imagining things. She *knew* Rodney. And if she had to search through every closet, drawer and photo album in this house, she'd figure out how she knew him.

She'd start tonight, during the cocktail party. There would be so many guests milling around the house, no one would notice if she slipped away for a few minutes. However, they would notice if she showed up at a formal cocktail party wearing denim.

She sighed, looking in despair at the wrinkled denim dress she'd worn for two days straight. Hardly appropriate for a formal party. But neither were the casual slacks and blouses Adam had purchased for her in Butte.

She directed a longing look at the beautiful silk window hanging. If she had Scarlett's ingenuity and a seamstress handy, she could probably turn the drapes into a killer cocktail dress. Or maybe she could wrap herself in the lacy bedspread, toga-style.

A knock on the door interrupted her design plans. "Come in."

Rodney walked through the door, his finger hooked around a hanger slung over his shoulder. "Your fairy godmother is here."

Katie's mouth dropped open as he held up a dress for her inspection. It was a simple satin sheath, the color of warm caramel. The iridescent fabric shimmered under the ceiling light.

"This is for me?" she asked at last.

Rodney nodded. "I noticed you didn't have any luggage with you, so I assumed you might need a dress for the party tonight. One of my old girlfriends left this here. There are also some size eight shoes to match."

She wore size eight and a half, but why quibble?

He looked from the dress to Katie. "I think you'll look perfect in it."

She couldn't wait to try it on. "Just give me a minute and you can see for yourself."

When she emerged from the dressing room, Rodney gave a low whistle. "Perfect doesn't begin to describe it."

Snug didn't begin to describe it. She had to move a certain way just to be able to breathe. But it was still an improvement over the drapes. "I don't know how to thank you."

He smiled. "I'll think of something."

His smiled nudged her memory once more. Maybe he did know her but just didn't remember. She took a step closer to him. "Rodney, you look so familiar to me. Is it possible we've met somewhere before?"

"You know, I do feel a connection between us." He reached out and tipped up her chin with one crooked finger, studying her face. "But I'm sure I'd never forget a woman like you."

"Am I interrupting something?" Adam stood in the open door, his arms folded.

Katie swallowed as she stepped away from Rodney. "We were just talking." Then she twirled once around. "Look what Rodney gave me."

"Maybe next time he could find a dress that's actually your size."

Rodney shrugged. "I had to guess her measurements, but I think it looks wonderful on her."

Adam stepped between them, facing Katie. "I'm going to check on Wiley. Would you like to come along?"

She nodded, then gave a small wave to Rodney

as Adam practically pulled her out the bedroom door. She followed him through the hallway and down the staircase, quickening her step to keep up with his long strides. He didn't say a word to her until they stepped out the front door of the house.

"We need to set some rules about this weekend." Gravel crunched beneath their shoes as they walked toward the stable.

The evening breeze blew wisps of hair on Katie's face, tickling her cheek until she brushed them back. "What kind of rules?"

"Number one is that you only get one bachelor for your money. Rodney is off limits."

Her eyes widened. "You think I'm interested in Rodney?"

A muscle ticked in his jaw. "Aren't you?"

She struggled for something rational to say. Rodney Tate did interest her, but for one reason and one reason only. He was the sole link to her past. "Certainly not for romance. The man is engaged."

"That's never stopped him before."

Katie blinked at him. "Are you jealous?"

"Of course not. I just don't like to walk in and find my best friend getting cozy with my date."

"It wasn't like that." Katie paused outside the stable door and turned to Adam. "I thanked him for the dress and..."

"That's another thing. That dress." His gaze raked over her, and the flash of heat in his eyes made her blush. "Don't you think it's just a little provocative?"

"I didn't pick it out," she retorted. "And it was either wear this or that denim dress with coyote slobber all over it." She spun and marched inside the stable. "I can't believe you think I'd betray you with your best friend. What kind of woman do you think I am?"

Adam stalked in after her. "I have no idea. You spread rumors about me to lower the price at the auction. You stowed away in the back seat of my car after I specifically forbade you from coming with me. You smacked me with a telephone."

She edged around a wheel barrow as she moved towards Wiley's pen. "That was an accident."

"Maybe." He grasped her elbow and whirled her around. "The point is you wanted *me*. You bought *me*. You got *me*. So I'd appreciate it if you'd act like it."

"Fine." Anger drove her right into his arms. She clamped her mouth over his in a possessive kiss that backed him clear up against a wooden support beam. She flung her arms around his neck, putting all her frustration and turmoil and pent-up passion into that kiss.

Obviously caught off balance by her sudden frontal attack, Adam recovered quickly. He wrapped his arms around her waist and pulled her off the floor. He groaned low in his throat as his mouth battled hers for possession.

Soon Katie couldn't tell which moans belonged to her and which belonged to Adam. He pulled her closer as he deepened the kiss. Katie's head tipped back as her anger melted away and hot, pulsing desire took its place.

Wiley's frantic yipping dragged her back from oblivion. She drew away from Adam, horrified by her actions. She'd practically attacked the man.

"I'm sorry," she said, trying to catch her breath. "I got carried away."

He swallowed, his Adam's apple bobbing in his throat. "No problem."

But it was a problem. A big problem. Her heart raced and her knees trembled and she could barely resist the impulse to kiss him again. Nothing was turning out right on this trip. She turned away from him, busying herself by filling Wiley's bowl with puppy chow. "I don't think we should let it happen again."

He didn't say anything for a long moment. "Why not? We're both consenting adults, and you did purchase me for a romantic weekend getaway."

She turned to face him. "We hardly know each other."

Adam's gaze fell to her mouth. "I know a way to remedy that."

Katie took a step back, almost tripping over Wiley's food dish. The coyote pup loudly gulped his dinner, oblivious to the tempest churning just a few feet above him. "I don't think that's a good idea."

"Are you playing games with me?"

"No," she whispered.

Adam stared at her, then turned toward the stable door. "We'd better go in if we don't want to miss the party."

She knew Adam didn't believe her, but this was anything but a game to her. Her future depended on what she discovered this weekend. Maybe her very life. She didn't intend to give up her search just because Rodney claimed not to know her. There had to be something in his house that would provide a clue to her identity.

And she intended to find it.

THAT EVENING, Adam mingled among the guests at the cocktail party without once taking his eyes off Katie. He told himself he didn't trust her. Told himself that as head of security for ExecTec, he needed to keep his eye on suspicious characters. But suspicion wasn't what drew his attention to her. It was the way that caramel dress melted around her body, leaving very little to the imagination. It was the way her hips gently swayed when she walked. It was those long, long legs.

A leggy redhead.

He mentally shook himself. It absolutely could not be the same woman. Katie was a waitress from a tiny town in Wyoming. She'd probably never been to Chicago, much less attempted to steal business information. She didn't even show any interest in stealing his heart.

Adam turned away from her, draining his champagne glass. She'd been avoiding him ever since that scorching kiss in the barn. His date had made it perfectly clear that she didn't want their relationship to progress any further.

So why the hell had she bought him in the first place?

That was the forty-seven dollar and fifty-five cent question. And he was determined to discover the answer, even if it took all weekend.

A paunchy, balding man sidled up to Adam. "I've got three words for you," the man said under his breath. "Powdered rhinoceros horn."

"Excuse me?" Adam looked around, certain the man must be speaking to someone else. But the closest party guests were gathered around the guacamole bowl five feet away.

"It works wonders," the man whispered. "It's a little costly, but a man can't put a price on his...hardware. If you know what I mean."

"Have we met?" Adam asked, looking askance at his champagne flute. He'd only had two glasses, but this conversation was making no sense at all. The man chuckled, then shook Adam's hand in his big, beefy paw. "Name's Sanders, Gaylen Sanders. Course we just go by first names in IA."

"IA?"

"Impotence Anonymous," Gaylen whispered. "I put your name up for membership after I read that story about you in the Montana *Standard* today."

A hot rush of blood crept up his neck. "There must be some mistake."

Gaylen shook his head. "No, sirree, there was your name and picture and everything. It was part of some human interest story about a charity bachelor auction to raise money for a boys' ranch down in Wyoming."

"Lost Springs," Adam muttered.

"That's it! Anyway, my wife liked it so much she thought we should donate a few dollars to a good cause."

"I'm sure they'd appreciate it," Adam said numbly. He couldn't believe it. A newspaper story. About him and his battle with impotence. With his luck, it probably hit the AP wire and made every newspaper across the country.

"You're looking a little peaked there, son," Gaylen said, his voice lowering in concern. "You feelin' all right?"

"I'm fine," Adam replied. "Perfectly fine."

"Take my word for it," Gaylen said, nudging Adam in the ribs. "You'll be a lot finer with some powdered rhinoceros horn. Now, don't you forget it." Then he headed for the guacamole bowl.

Unfortunately, Adam doubted he could forget it if he tried. Especially since it was now spelled out in black and white for all the world to see. Thanks to a certain waitress. He spotted Katie instantly across the room. She was hard to miss in that dress. And it made him feel anything but impotent. Adam began walking toward her when Rodney stepped in his path.

"Time to turn on the charm," Rodney said out of the side of his mouth. "We've got a potential business investor heading our way."

Adam swallowed a groan of frustration. "Who is it?"

"Lorene Baker. She's an estate attorney. She also happens to be my future mother-in-law."

Adam watched a stately, older woman approach them, her ash blond hair swept up in an elegant chignon. She wore a chic black cocktail dress and an air of sophistication.

"Hello, Lorene," Rodney greeted her, leaning over to kiss her sculptured cheek. "I'd like you to meet a friend of mine."

"Don't tell me," Lorene interjected, her cool blue eyes assessing Adam, "let me guess. You're Adam Harper."

Rodney laughed. "How did you know?"

"She probably reads the newspapers," Adam muttered.

"I did happen to catch your story in this morning's edition,'' Lorene affirmed. ''I applaud your courage in participating in that bachelor auction, despite your...disability. Didn't a cleaning woman buy you?''

''A waitress,'' Adam amended. ''Katie O'Hara from Lightning Creek, Wyoming.''

''Katie is Adam's date for the wedding,'' Rodney said, pointing her out to Lorene. Katie stood next to the baby grand piano, conversing with Gaylen Sanders.

Lorene's gaze swept over Katie, and Adam detected a hint of disapproval in her expression. Obviously, he wasn't the only one who thought she shouldn't be dressed like that in public.

''It's all really quite...fascinating,'' Lorene said, still staring at Katie.

''That's one word for it,'' Adam replied. ''Not exactly the one I would use....''

''Am I missing something here?'' Rodney interjected.

''Your fiancée,'' Lorene said smoothly, turning her attention to him. ''I can't find my daughter anywhere. She really should be here to greet your guests.''

Rodney grinned. ''Darla's probably still up in her room fixing her hair. She drove back from Butte with the top down on the convertible.''

Lorene pressed her lips together. ''If you'll excuse me, gentlemen, I'll just run upstairs and hurry her along.''

Rodney waited until Lorene left the room before he turned to Adam. ''I hit the jackpot.''

''With Darla or her mother?''

''Both. Lorene was recently named trustee of the

Devlin estate. Old man Devlin left millions behind when he died a few months ago. Now she's got all that money to invest. What better risk than her new son-in-law's company?''

"I thought Devlin had children. Wouldn't they inherit?''

Rodney shook his head. "Devlin's daughter had a heart condition and passed away several years ago. And his son died or was disowned or something. Anyway, as soon as the probate clears, I think we should approach Lorene with a tempting investment opportunity at ExecTec.''

Adam sipped his drink. "Does Darla mind mixing business with family?''

"Darla doesn't know a thing about it. And I'd like to keep it that way.''

"Sounds like a great way to start a marriage.''

"Well, I don't want her to think I'm marrying her for her money.''

"Are you?''

Rodney ignored the question, elbowing past Adam as a petite brunette with a shy smile appeared in the doorway. "There's my Muffin." Rodney ushered her into the room. "Adam, I'd like you to meet my fiancée, Darla Baker. Darla, this is Adam Harper.''

"Nice to meet you, Adam." Dark lashes fringed her blue eyes, and her small nose tilted slightly upward.

Adam found himself pleasantly surprised by fiancée number five. The previous fiancées in Rodney's collection had all been Barbie dolls. This woman looked not only somewhat intelligent, but radiantly happy. "It's a pleasure to meet you, Darla.''

She smiled. "Tater's spoken so highly of you."

Adam looked at Rodney. "Tater?"

A red flush mantled Rodney's sallow cheeks. "It's her nickname for me."

Darla laughed. "I call him Tater instead of Tate. And he calls me Muffin, because my last name is Baker. Get it?"

"Got it," Adam replied as Rodney turned crimson. "So how did you two meet?"

Rodney gazed at his fiancée. "By accident. Literally. She backed her car into mine at the Marriott hotel parking lot in Denver. I was there speaking at a software symposium, and Darla was there having lunch with her mother." He chuckled. "She made quite an impression on me...and my car."

Darla elbowed him playfully in the ribs. "Very funny." Then she turned to Adam. "Tater tells me you were his bodyguard during those awful years at that boys' ranch."

"He still protects me," Rodney asserted. "Adam has this whole place wired with a state-of-the-art security system. He'll probably check you out, too, Muffin, just to make sure you're not an industrial spy."

Darla paled.

"Don't worry," Adam assured her. "It's a painless procedure."

Rodney wrapped his arm around her waist. "She's too cute to be a spy. Speaking of cute, where's your date?"

Adam looked around the room, searching through the crowd for his leggy redhead.

But Katie O'Hara was nowhere in sight.

KATIE ONLY GOT LOST twice searching for Rodney's study. The house was a maze of rooms and nooks and storage closets, all closed behind identical solid oak doors. She discovered his study was one of the few rooms on the lower level that wasn't locked. Ostensibly because it contained none of the valuable secrets of ExecTec.

Katie slipped inside, closing the door behind her, then locking it just in case somebody else wanted to snoop around. Scarlett O'Hara had never resorted to snooping in someone else's house in the one thousand thirty-seven pages of *Gone With the Wind.* However, she had killed a Yankee, hidden his body and married her sister's fiancé. Comparatively speaking, snooping seemed pretty minor.

Still, she didn't feel comfortable in here. One reason for that was the torture devices on her feet. Not only were her shoes a half size too small, they were made for a woman with no toes.

She kicked them off, then leaned back against the wall, propping one foot on her thigh to rub her numb toes. Her gaze scanned the room, noting the backlit oak bookshelves, the massive oak desk in the middle of the room and the set of three filing cabinets in one corner. She massaged the toes of her other foot, then checked her watch. She didn't want to be absent from the party for more than fifteen minutes. Five minutes had already been wasted finding the room, which meant she'd have to hurry.

She walked across the plush beige carpet, her sore toes sinking thankfully into the padded softness. She pulled open the top desk drawer, wincing at the slight squeal of the metal rollers. Her heart pounded a rapid tattoo in her chest as she drew the desk lamp closer. She'd kept the overhead lights in Rodney's study off, not wanting to attract attention. She could hear the rumble of voices through the wall vent and knew the party was in full swing. It was the perfect opportunity to conduct her search.

She rifled through the drawer, pulling out a black leather-bound address book. She flipped through the names, not knowing if her own was printed among them. With a stifled groan of frustration, she replaced the address book and sifted through the rest of the drawer's contents. All she found was a collection of comic books, a chocolate chip cookie and a hand-held computer game.

She moved to the bookshelf, hoping to find a photo album or perhaps a college yearbook. Rodney did have some memorabilia on the middle shelf, including a signed baseball, a University of Wyoming football pennant and a slightly lopsided green ceramic pot. Several loose Polaroid photographs were inside the pot. Katie pulled them out and quickly flipped through them, looking for anything familiar.

She found it.

A photograph of Adam Harper with a svelte blonde wrapped around him. The festive wreath in the background proclaimed it the scene of a Christmas party. The blonde's state of undress showed she'd obviously had too much eggnog.

And he accused her of playing fast and loose?

An unexpected and totally inappropriate stab of jealousy pricked her. She wanted to rip that blonde off Adam by her bleached roots.

"Looking for something?" The office lights flipped on.

Katie jumped, then whirled. The picture dropped

from her hand and fluttered to the carpet. "Adam, I was just..."

He walked across the room and knelt to pick it up. With an expression she could only describe as nostalgic, he gazed at the photograph. *The jerk.* If he was going to drool over another woman, he could at least have the courtesy to do it when she wasn't around. Not that she was jealous. Far from it. She was actually glad it was distracting him. Really.

"That was some Christmas party," he said at last.

"So who is she?" Katie asked, suppressing the urge to rip the photograph out of his hands.

Adam crinkled his brow. "I know this sounds awful, but I honestly can't remember her name."

Maybe Katie's amnesia was contagious. Or maybe he'd had so many women in his life, he couldn't keep track of them all.

Adam flipped the picture over in his hand. "This was taken a couple of years ago. Where did you find it?"

"In the pot."

He turned to the potted palm in the corner. "Did you have to dig for it?"

"Not that pot," she said, then pointed at the bookshelf behind him.

Adam stared at it for a moment, then slowly walked to the shelf. He took the green ceramic pot down, holding it in his big hands. "I can't believe it's still in one piece."

"It looks hand-crafted."

A smile quirked up one side of his mouth as he turned the crude pottery in his hands. "Is that a polite way of saying it's less than perfect?"

"I like it," Katie replied, being less than perfect

herself. Then she saw the initials carved in the bottom. "What does A.M.H. stand for?"

"Adam Monroe Harper."

She looked at him in surprise. "You made this?"

"A long time ago," he replied, letting her take it out of his hands. "I must have been about thirteen. Pottery was one of the required courses at Lost Springs. I made it for…my mother. Green was her favorite color."

She smoothed her hand over the slick green surface, imagining Adam's fingers painstakingly molding and shaping the pot. Judging by the fine detail etched in the clay, he must have spent hours on it. "It's beautiful."

"It's the ugliest thing I've ever seen," he said bluntly. "It belongs in the trash. In fact, that's where I put it until Rodney dug it out." He shook his head. "I can't believe he still has it after all these years."

Katie wanted to know why his mother didn't have it. Did she reject it the way she'd rejected her son? The questions burned in the back of her throat. But what right did she have to question him about his past? Especially when she didn't have the answers to her own?

He quirked an eyebrow. "So have I given you enough time?"

"Time for what?"

"To think up a good excuse for why you're prowling around Rodney's study."

"I wouldn't call it prowling."

"The door was locked and the lights were off. Of course, darkness won't hamper an infrared security camera."

"A camera?" Her blood turned cold. She knew

as soon as Adam and Rodney saw the images of her searching through the desk, they'd boot her right out of the house.

He withdrew a small canister from his tuxedo pocket. "Unfortunately, I'll have to explain to Rodney once again that the security camera doesn't do any good without film in it."

She breathed a silent sigh of relief. "You mean there's no film in the camera?"

His gaze fell to her mouth. "Nope. So you're safe in case you feel an overwhelming urge to kiss me again."

Safe didn't come close to describing how kissing Adam made her feel. Hot. Bothered. Confused. Even those words couldn't define the experience. "Thanks, but no thanks."

He folded his arms across his chest. "Then maybe you'd like to finally tell me what you're doing in here."

She swallowed. "Rodney asked me to meet him here. He wanted my recipe for barbecue sauce."

Adam stepped closer, and she could see the dangerous glint in his blue eyes. "So where is he? Hiding in the desk drawer?"

She looked at the drawer she'd inadvertently left standing open. "No, of course not. I...was looking for some paper and a pen to leave him a note."

"There's a notepad on the desk."

She glanced at the immaculate desktop. "Oh...I must have missed it."

He stood next to her as she picked up a pen off the desk and began scribbling on the notepad. She was so intent on keeping her hand from shaking, she barely knew what she was writing. She tore off the top sheet from the notepad and folded it in half.

Without a word, Adam reached out his hand for it. Katie hesitated a moment, then passed it to him. But instead of reading it, he placed it in the pocket of his suit coat. "Darla would like to meet you."

Katie nodded, then led the way out of the room, Adam close on her heels. She didn't want to imagine what he must think of her. What ugly reasons he might suspect for her presence in Rodney's private office. Whatever he might think, she couldn't tell him the truth. Not yet. Not until she had the answers to her questions.

Someone had tried to kill her two months ago. Someone from her past. Rodney Tate was connected to her past, and Adam was connected to Rodney. It was a tangled mess leaving her unable to trust anyone but herself.

When they reached the party room, Adam clasped her elbow and steered her toward Rodney. His touch was cool impersonal. Suppressing a shiver, she looked at him. "Adam, I...."

"Later," he growled.

She looked away from him, letting her gaze wander over the party guests. A small knot of men were engaged in an intense conversation about the flagrant abuses of software copyright. A woman wearing silver sequins played soft jazz on the baby grand piano under the chandelier. Uniformed waiters carried trays of sparkling champagne and hors d'oeuvres.

When they reached the love seat, Rodney and a pert brunette rose to greet them. Rodney smiled at

Katie, his gaze openly admiring her clinging dress. Adam's fingertips flexed on her elbow.

"We thought you'd gotten lost, Katie," Rodney said, slipping his arm around Darla's waist.

So much for her lame excuse of meeting Rodney in his study.

"But I knew Adam could track you down. He's an expert at that sort of thing." Rodney turned to the woman at his side. "Muffin, this is Katie O'Hara. She bought Adam at the Lost Springs bachelor auction. So now he's completely at her mercy."

Darla stared slack-jawed at Katie.

"It's a new experience for both of us." Katie managed a laugh, aware of her bachelor standing stiff and solemn by her side. Then she held out her hand. "It's nice to meet you, Darla. And congratulations on finding a bachelor the old fashioned way."

Darla's gaze fell to Katie's outstretched hand, then she dropped into a dead faint.

CHAPTER SEVEN

"YOU REALLY HAVE a way with people," Adam said as Rodney carried his fiancée from the room. Darla had come to quickly, claiming the wine had made her dizzy and she just needed a little rest.

"It's not my fault," Katie insisted, but her heart was hammering in her chest. Because it was her fault. Darla had *recognized* her. She was sure of it. Katie could barely keep herself from running after Rodney and his semiconscious fiancée.

"I didn't say it was your fault," Adam countered. "I'm just amazed at the effect you have on people. First Rodney, now Darla."

"How about you?"

He took a step closer to her. "Especially me."

Her breathing hitched. "Adam, about before..."

"Careful, Katie," he said softly. "There's something you should know about me. I hate lies. Any kind of lies. So if you're not ready to tell me the truth, don't say anything at all."

She closed her mouth. She'd lied to him from the moment she'd bought him. And she still couldn't tell him anything...yet. If she confided to him now, she'd probably find herself booted out of the house with his big footprint on her rear end. Besides, Adam Harper knew everything about her he needed to know. Almost as much as she knew herself.

She licked her dry lips. "So you're just going to forget...about before?"

He took a sip of the cocktail in his hand. "I'll do what I have to do."

Katie pressed her lips together. Another cryptic answer. For a man who hated lies, he skirted around the truth enough himself when it suited him. Still, he'd kept her little excursion to himself. She touched his forearm. "Thank you, Adam. I appreciate it. And in case you're wondering, you *can* trust me."

"Actually, I was wondering if I could trust myself."

She gazed into his sky blue eyes, but before she could reply, he set down his drink and pulled her onto the dance floor. Her breath caught in her throat as he held her close to him, his body moving sinuously against hers.

She panicked for one brief moment, uncertain if she knew how to dance. But her feet moved naturally to the sultry rhythm of the rumba. Or maybe she just floated in Adam's arms. He seemed so competent and sure of himself. At that moment, Katie thought she might follow him anywhere.

"Have you ever been to Chicago?"

The question surprised her, causing her to hesitate a moment before she replied. "Not that I can remember. Why?"

"Just curious." His warm breath caressed her ear, sending a delicious shock wave through her body.

The music changed to a soft, slow beat. He slid both hands to her hips, and she draped her arms around his neck. She inhaled the spicy scent of his aftershave as his jaw nestled against her cheek. She closed her eyes, enjoying the moment. Enjoying it way too much.

She was wasting time. Instead of dancing, she should seek out Darla and find out if it was the wine that had caused her to faint or the sight of Katie standing in front of her.

But she couldn't seem to leave Adam's arms. It was as if they drifted in their own little cocoon apart from the rest of the world. An alien world that didn't seem to have a place for her in it. A world she didn't want to worry about for the next five minutes.

Adam pulled her closer, his hips brushing against hers. Heat sizzled between them. Katie gazed into his eyes, not surprised at the desire swirling in those blue depths. They mirrored her own.

"I'm definitely going to miss you," he said huskily.

She blinked. "Miss me?"

"When you leave tomorrow."

She stiffened in his arms. "Where am I going?"

"Back to Lightning Creek. Our weekend ends tomorrow."

"But I've hardly had time to...get to know you." *Or time to know myself.* She couldn't leave tomorrow with all her questions still unanswered. If Rodney didn't know her, Darla certainly did. She'd looked at Katie as if she'd seen a ghost. Only Katie was very real, and had no intention of disappearing.

Adam shrugged. "According to the bachelor auction rules, your money is good for one weekend only." He arched a brow. "You always play by the rules, don't you, Katie?"

She could hear the undercurrent in his tone. Adam didn't trust her. And why should he, after catching her red-handed in Rodney's office? She nibbled her lower lip, wondering what to do next.

"I'll drive you into Butte in the morning," he offered. "I'll even buy you an airplane ticket."

He obviously couldn't wait to be rid of her. For some reason, that bothered her more than anything. "That won't be necessary."

"I insist." His cool tone contradicted the sensuous movements of his body.

"What about Wiley?"

"I'll make sure he's taken care of until he's completely healed."

"You'll have to watch him," she warned. "He's already figured out how to unlatch the gate to his pen. And check his stitches every day to make certain there's no infection."

"He'll be fine," Adam murmured, his tone softer. She nestled her head against his shoulder while her mind raced for an excuse, any excuse, to stay. "I'd like to be here for the wedding."

He pulled back far enough to look at her. "That's three days from now."

"I've been meaning to ask you why they're getting married on a Wednesday. Isn't that a little unusual?"

"It's because the first three letters of Wednesday are W-E-D."

She smiled. "Unusual, but romantic. So what do you say?"

The music stopped, and Adam stepped away from her, a muscle knotting his jaw. "I say no." Then he turned and walked out the door.

ADAM WANTED HER to stay. It was stupid, illogical and most of all dangerous, but it was true. He just couldn't figure out why. He shouldn't want to be stuck in Montana with a woman who drove him to distraction. A woman he couldn't trust, no matter how passionate her kisses to convince him otherwise.

That should be his first clue that Katie O'Hara might not be the innocent, wide-eyed waitress she pretended to be. Was it possible his waitress was really the woman the doorman had seen outside Adam's apartment? He thrust his fingers through his hair. He felt confused and tired and, most of all, frustrated by that slow burn he'd shared with Katie on the dance floor.

Just another indication he was playing with fire.

Rodney stuck his head in the door. "You wanted to see me?"

Adam motioned him into the study. "Close the door behind you."

Rodney glanced at his watch as he stepped into the room. "Make it quick. I don't want to leave Darla alone for too long."

It was well after midnight. A few party stragglers remained in the house, trying their best to finish off the premium champagne.

"How is she?"

"To tell you the truth, she's acting a little strange. I think the stress of the wedding must be getting to her. I've given her orders not to leave her bed."

Adam arched a brow. "Does she follow orders?"

Rodney grinned. "Not usually, but she's not fighting me on this one. Which proves she's been under too much stress." He tugged at the bow tie around his neck. "Now, why did you want to see me?"

Adam didn't quite know where to begin. "We need to talk."

"So talk." Rodney sidled around the desk and seated himself in the armchair. He folded his arms behind his head and propped his feet on top of the desk.

Adam remained standing. "I caught someone going through your desk earlier this evening."

Rodney lowered his feet to the floor. "Tell me you're joking."

Adam shook his head. "As far as I can tell, nothing was taken. But you might want to double-check."

Rodney pulled open his desk drawers, sifting through the contents. At last he said, "My chocolate chip cookie is gone."

"I got hungry waiting for you."

"Well, everything else seems to be here." He looked at Adam. "Why would someone go through my desk? I don't keep any programming or technical information in this room. I don't even keep the door to this room locked."

Adam shrugged. "I'm not entirely convinced the perpetrator was after industry information."

Rodney snorted. "The guy had to be after something. Frankly, I don't like the idea of someone snooping through my belongings. Who was it?"

Adam tensed. "The who isn't as important as the why."

"It's important to me. Just give me a name. It had to be one of the guests at the party tonight."

"I need to do a little more investigating first,"

Adam replied, suddenly reluctant to reveal Katie's duplicity. He wasn't certain why he was protecting her. One word and Rodney would have her in handcuffs. Despite how attractive he might find her, Rodney was terrified of corporate espionage. "You just worry about the wedding and Darla."

"All right." Rodney rose out of his chair. "I'm sure you can handle it." No doubt he had faith Adam would get him out of this trouble, just as he'd always done in the past.

Adam intended to do just that, even if it meant betraying Katie. *Betraying?* He blinked at the odd emotion that word stirred inside him. How could he betray a woman he barely knew? And why did he feel this primal instinct to protect her?

"Oh, by the way," Rodney said as he stood in the doorway. "I have a surprise for you."

Adam groaned inwardly. Rodney's last surprise had been a pet iguana. "What is it?"

"It's not a what, it's a who. Sam's coming to the wedding."

"Sam?" Adam echoed.

"Sam Duncan from Lost Springs. I sent him an invitation, but I never thought he'd come all the way up here. He must be getting pretty old by now."

Adam nodded as the wheels turned in his head. Maybe Sam could fill in the details about Katie O'Hara. After all, they both lived in the same small town. Maybe she was simply a harmless, sexy waitress who just happened to fit the description of a leggy redhead.

But he had to be sure. After Rodney left, Adam picked up the telephone receiver and dialed the Chicago area code, followed by the phone number of one of his most trusted employees. "Corinne, this is Harper. I want you to find out everything you can about a woman named Katie O'Hara from Lightning Creek, Wyoming."

KATIE CREPT ALONG the dim, narrow hallway hoping Darla wouldn't faint again when she saw her. A middle-of-the-night meeting might seem a little dramatic, but Adam hadn't given her much choice. She had to see Darla, and she had to do it tonight.

She reached the pair of double doors at the end of the hallway. Darla's room. At least, she thought it was Darla's room. She held her breath and turned the brass doorknob, wincing as the door creaked open. She stepped inside, then closed it quickly behind her, her blue cotton nightgown floating around her ankles. Then she moved toward the bed. The empty bed.

Turning back the covers, she stared at the unwrinkled satin bedsheets. Darla obviously hadn't been resting. Her stomach twisted as a new thought occurred to her. Had the sight of Katie scared her away? Had Darla taken off for good?

"Get real, O'Hara," she muttered to herself. The woman was getting married in three days. It would take something monumental for her to go AWOL from her own wedding. *Something like the return of a woman she thought dead?*

"Katie?"

Startled, she turned to see Rodney walk out of the bathroom, a Snoopy toothbrush in his hand. He wore Snoopy boxer shorts and a worn red T-shirt.

"What are you doing in here?" he asked, his gaze falling to the pulled-back sheets.

"Rodney, I..."

"No, don't say it." He hurried over to her, clasping his hand over her mouth. His fingers smelled like tartar-control Crest. "I've seen the way you look at me, Katie. But this is a mistake. A big mistake."

With his hand still firmly against her mouth, her attempts to explain came out in an incoherent jabber.

"I'll admit I'm attracted to you, too," he said, stepping closer to her. "But I can't betray my best friend or my fiancée. We have to stay strong, Katie." His gaze flicked to the elastic neckline of her nightgown, then he closed his eyes. "We have to resist temptation."

At the moment she was tempted to kick him in the shin. He actually thought she'd come here to seduce him! She jerked away from him and opened her mouth to tell him the truth—she'd been on her way to Darla's room and simply gotten lost. But she bit down on her tongue in time. He'd want to know why she'd been skulking around his house searching for Darla's room in the middle of the night.

"I know what you're going to say," Rodney said as he watched her internal struggle.

She sincerely hoped not. He wouldn't let her within one hundred feet of his fiancée if he knew Katie was the cause of Darla's dizzy spell.

"You're going to tell me I'm rushing into this marriage," he continued. "That Darla and I have only known each other a few short weeks. You wonder how I can be sure she's the right woman, the only woman, for me."

"How *can* you be sure?" Katie asked, playing along.

"Good question," he said, grasping her shoulders. "There's only one way to find out."

Then he kissed her.

Katie froze as his wet, minty mouth assaulted her lips. She forced herself to stand there, eyes open, until he broke the kiss. *Maybe now he'd remember her.*

Rodney turned away with a groan. "I knew it. I knew I wouldn't be able to resist your advances." He buried his face in his hands. "This is a disaster."

He looked so distraught, she reached out to pat his shoulder. "I think you're overreacting. It was just a little kiss."

He lifted his head to stare at her. "That doesn't matter. Don't you see? I just *kissed* another woman. That proves I'm not totally committed to Darla. I don't deserve a woman like her."

"Why don't we both just forget it ever happened."

Hope flashed in his eyes. "Do you think you can do that?"

"Believe me, I've got a rotten memory."

"All right," he agreed. "We'll pretend it never happened. But just to be safe, I think we should avoid being alone together."

"I can live with that."

"Just forget all about me, Katie. Concentrate on Adam." Then he paled. "Just don't tell him what happened. If he ever found out about that kiss, he'd beat me to a pulp."

"I won't tell him," Katie said. "On one condition."

"Name it."

"Invite me to stay for the wedding. I could help

out in the kitchen or wherever you need me. I've got a lot of experience with catering for large crowds.''

''Actually, that's not a bad idea,'' Rodney mused. ''It might take some of the burden off Darla if you could supervise the kitchen staff and coordinate all the last-minute details.''

''Then let me stay. Adam plans to put me on a plane to Lightning Creek tomorrow, but I don't want to go.''

Rodney sighed. ''Maybe it would be for the best.''

''It wouldn't be best for me,'' she said, desperately. Then she began to improvise. ''Besides, Adam may be just the man to help me get over you. He and I could spend more time together and really get to know each other.''

''He is a great guy. And this could be kind of a test for me.''

''A test?''

He nodded. ''If I can't stay completely true to Darla over the next couple of days, then I'll know the wedding is a mistake and call it off.''

Katie didn't know if she wanted to be the bait for Rodney's fidelity test, but what choice did she have? ''I know you can do it.''

He took a deep breath. ''I hope so.'' Then he frowned at her. ''It would probably help if you weren't standing in my bedroom in your nightgown.''

She took the hint and headed toward the door, resisting the urge to do cartwheels. *Three more days in Montana.*

Scarlett O'Hara would be proud of her.

Adam Harper would be furious.

CHAPTER EIGHT

EARLY MONDAY MORNING Katie went to the stables to check on Wiley. He'd unlatched the gate to his pen again and engaged in a spirited game of hide-and-seek with her. She finally caught him behind a stack of fresh straw bales.

"You're one ornery coyote," she said as she checked the stitches on his belly. A little redness and swelling surrounded the wound, but the veterinarian had said that was normal. He certainly acted normal, and he was definitely living up to his name.

"Now you stay put," she said, setting him in his pen and latching the gate once again. He ran straight for the bowl of puppy chow. She sighed as she watched him scarf down his breakfast. "What am I going to do with you?"

"Good question."

Katie turned to see Adam leaning in the stable doorway, his hands tucked into his pants pockets. He wore faded blue jeans and a chambray shirt. The long sleeves were pushed up to his elbows, revealing tanned, sinewy forearms. A heartbreaker in a tuxedo or in denim. The man would look good in anything. *Or nothing.* Heat suffused her cheeks as she imagined Adam Harper au naturel. She was wrong. He'd look even better in nothing.

She swallowed hard. "Is something wrong?"

He stalked toward her. "Something's been wrong ever since I met you. If it's not a car, it's a coyote. Or a bride-to-be who faints at the sight of you."

"How is Darla this morning?"

"Darla's fine, although she refuses to leave her room. How do you explain that?"

"Wedding jitters. It's normal for a bride to be nervous before the ceremony. I've agreed to help out in any way I can until Darla is back on her feet."

He took a step closer to her, his blue eyes narrowing. "That's another thing."

Katie forced herself not to retreat. Strength and heat emanated from him. He stood so near she could smell the fresh scent of soap on his skin.

"How did you talk Rodney into letting you stay for the wedding?"

"He invited me. I'm not sure exactly how it came up in the conversation—"

"Save it, O'Hara." His gaze fell on her mouth. "We both know you have ways of getting what you want."

Her cheeks warmed. "Just what are you implying?"

"I'm not implying anything. I'm saying loud and clear that this setup is all a little too cozy. Rodney can't stop talking about you. It's Katie this and Katie that."

A new and totally unexpected thought occurred to her. "Are you jealous?"

"*Jealous?*" He laughed. "You think I'm jealous?"

His amusement made her bristle. Especially when she remembered her own stab of jealousy after seeing that photograph of Adam tangled up with a willowy blonde. "Why else would you be all…hot and bothered?"

His blue eyes flashed, and a curl of anticipation unfurled in Katie's stomach. He was dynamite, and she was playing with matches. He took another step closer to her, and she braced herself for the explosion.

"Now," Adam said, his voice low and dangerous, "let's get something straight. I am not jealous."

She tipped up her chin. "Then what are you?"

"Suspicious."

Her heart skipped a beat. "I already told you I'm not interested in Rodney."

"Then what does interest you, Katie?"

She licked her lips. "I'm not sure what you mean."

"If that question is too hard, let's try another one." He advanced toward her. "Why were you so anxious to come with me to Montana?"

"I needed a vacation," she said, retreating until she was backed up against Wiley's pen.

"What were you looking for in Rodney's desk?"

"I already told you. A piece of paper."

He braced one hand on the post to her right, effectively blocking any escape. "A piece of paper with security codes on it, perhaps?"

She blinked at him in surprise. "What are you talking about?"

He studied her face, as if uncertain about what he saw there. "A couple of months ago, a woman described as a leggy redhead tried to weasel her way into my apartment in Chicago. Someone did manage to steal information from the personnel files at ExecTec."

"What does that have to do with me?"

His gaze flicked over her. "You're a redhead and you've got great legs."

She didn't know if she should take that as a compliment or an insult. "You think *I'm* the one responsible for the missing files and the attempted break-in?"

"You do fit the description."

She rolled her eyes. "Along with literally thousands of other women. Did you ever think of checking for fingerprints?"

"She didn't leave any prints behind. It was a professional job."

"Adam, I'm a waitress, remember? And not a very good one. I can assure you that I'm not a professional thief and I'm certainly not the woman you're looking for." She couldn't tell if he looked disappointed or relieved. She also couldn't tell him the truth. Not when he already suspected her of deceiving him. He lowered his hand from the post and took a step back, giving her room to breathe.

"Is that why you want me to leave today," she asked, "because you think I'm a security threat to your company?"

He reached out his hand to pull a piece of straw from her hair, his fingers caressing her jawline. "No," he replied, his voice husky, "that's not the reason."

Before she could react, Rodney walked through the stable door. "Hey, I've been looking everywhere for you two."

"Is there a problem?" Adam asked, dropping his hand and stepping away from her. Katie released the breath she didn't know she'd been holding.

Rodney grinned. "Just thc opposite. My fiancée is feeling much better."

"That is good news," Katie replied, forcing her attention away from Adam. "Is she up to having visitors yet?"

"Funny you should ask," Rodney said. "Darla wants to see you. In fact, she insists on it."

KATIE AND RODNEY walked together through the twists and turns of the second-story hallway. She still didn't know her way around the sprawling Tate mansion, and this journey was making her dizzy. Or maybe it was the apprehension of finally meeting someone who knew her.

"I hope Darla is feeling better," Katie said, breaking the awkward silence between them.

"Much better," Rodney replied. "It was the wine. She drinks too much when she's nervous, and it makes her dizzy. The same thing happened on our first date."

"She fainted on your date?"

He nodded, a nostalgic smile curving his mouth. "It scared me to death. I insisted she let me take her to the emergency room, even though she claimed she was fine. It was a Saturday night, so the place was packed. We sat there, just talking, for three hours while we waited for a doctor to see her." He turned to Katie as they reached the door to Darla's room. "It was the best date of my life."

Katie was so nervous she barely heard him. So many questions filled her mind. Why didn't Katie recognize Darla? Why had Darla fainted when she saw her? An odd foreboding flashed through her. Amnesia had erased everything from her past, both the good and the bad. Maybe there was a reason she didn't want to remember the bad. Maybe she'd be better off not knowing.

Katie shook herself. She couldn't let her fears stop her from learning the truth. Nothing was worse than this limbo she'd lived in for the past two months. Nothing.

She took a deep breath, ready to face her future. But Rodney's hand came down over hers, preventing her from turning the doorknob.

"Wait a minute," he whispered, "I have to tell you something."

Katie bit down on her lip to keep from screaming at the delay. "What?"

Rodney nervously licked his lips. "Darla is the possessive type."

She waited, but he didn't elaborate. "And?" she finally prompted.

"And she wouldn't understand about that little kiss we shared last night."

Katie studied him thoughtfully. "But we already agreed to forget about it."

"We did. I just want to make certain you know it didn't really mean anything." Rodney raked his hands through his thinning hair. "Sometimes I get confused about what I want. But I *know* I want Darla." He looked into Katie's eyes. "Do you understand?"

"Of course." She waited for him to open the door, but Rodney still didn't look convinced.

"Will you give me your word not to say anything to her about what happened last night?"

"Nothing happened last night."

He lowered his voice. "I know we didn't sleep together, but what about the kiss?"

She blinked innocently at him. "What kiss?"

Rodney's mouth curved into a slow grin. "You're quite a woman, Katie O'Hara. No wonder Adam is nuts over you."

Her pulse quickened. "He said that?"

"Not in so many words. But I know him pretty well." He turned toward the door. "Are you ready? We'd better not keep Darla waiting any longer."

Katie lightly touched his sleeve. "Rodney, I won't tell Darla what happened the other night. I give you my word."

Relief washed over his face. "Thank you. The longer I know you, the better I like you, Katie. And I know Darla will like you, too. She's already asked me so many questions about you."

That intrigued her. "What kind of questions?"

He shrugged. "The basics. Your name and where you're from and who invited you to the wedding. She wanted to know all about you." He swung open the door. "Now she can ask you herself."

Katie walked into the bedroom. It was even more lavish than her own. Rose satin drapes hung over the arched window. A matching comforter covered the round bed, which was centered on a platform in the middle of the room. In the bed was Darla, half-reclined, her straight, dark hair spilling over the white satin pillows behind her.

"Here she is," Rodney announced. He walked to the bed and placed his palm against Darla's forehead. "You look flushed. Are you sure you don't want me to call a doctor?"

"Positive," Darla replied, not taking her eyes off Katie.

Katie slowly walked forward. "I hope you're feeling better."

"Much better, thank you." Darla glanced at her fiancé. "Would you mind getting me some water, Tater?"

"Of course, Muffin." Rodney stroked the hair off her forehead. "Would you like Perrier or Evian?"

She shrugged. "Either one is fine."

He leaned over to kiss her, then turned to Katie. "Can I get you anything?"

"No, thank you."

Neither woman said a word until Rodney left the room. Then Darla sighed. "Isn't he wonderful?"

That wasn't exactly how Katie would describe a man who made passes at other women. But she didn't want to discuss Rodney. She wanted to know all about…herself. She moved to the side of the bed. "Rodney said you wanted to see me."

Darla picked at the satin threads in the coverlet. "I wanted to apologize for fainting like I did. It wasn't exactly the best…first impression." The last two words lingered in the air, almost like a question.

Katie was tired of playing games. "But haven't we met before?"

"No," Darla said, her voice firm. "We've never met." She stared out the window. "I don't know you and you don't know me. Agreed?"

Katie lowered herself onto the settee next to the bed. "No."

Darla tipped up her chin as she turned her gaze to Katie. "Then I'll have Rodney toss you out of here. I don't know what kind of game you're playing, but this is my life. I'm not going to let anyone screw it up."

"How could I possibly screw it up?"

"You know exactly how. Besides, I've seen the way he looks at you." Her blue eyes narrowed. "I may be in love, but I'm not blind. I know Rodney's a little weak where women are concerned. But I won't let you have him."

Katie rolled her eyes. "I don't want your fiancé."

"Then why else are you here?" Her words held suspicion...and something else. Fear. But what did Darla possibly have to fear from her?

"I'm here as Adam Harper's date," she said slowly.

Darla looked as if she really wanted to believe her. "And that's all?"

"What else is there?"

Darla shrugged. Katie bit her lip, knowing she couldn't let this opportunity pass her by. Darla knew something, Katie could sense it.

"What if I told you I really don't know you?" Katie said softly. "What if I told you I don't know anybody...including myself."

Darla's eyes widened. "I think you'd better go."

She leaned forward, her voice low. "Will you please tell me how you know me? At least tell me my name."

Darla shrank back against her pillow. "Okay, you're starting to scare me."

"I think I scared you the first time you saw me. Isn't that why you fainted?"

"It was the wine." Darla licked her pale lips. "Really."

Katie exhaled in frustration. She wasn't getting

anywhere. And Rodney could return at any moment. "Look, Darla, I know we've met before. Just remind me where and when."

This time there wasn't any fear in Darla's eyes, only confusion. "We've never met before. I swear."

Katie stood up, confused by the honest ring of truth in her words. "We haven't? Are you positive about that?"

Darla nodded emphatically.

"Then how…" Katie's voice trailed off as Rodney barreled into the room carrying an ice bucket filled with different varieties of bottled water.

"Here's your water, Muffin." He set the ice bucket on the small table beside the bed. "So has Katie spilled the secret yet?"

Darla choked on the water. When she recovered her breath she glanced nervously at Katie. "What secret?"

Rodney grinned. "She's agreed to help out with the wedding."

Darla's shoulders relaxed. "That really isn't necessary. It will just be a small, private ceremony."

Katie didn't miss her emphasis on the word *private*. "I have some catering experience, so Rodney asked me to help supervise the kitchen staff."

"I *really* don't want you to go to any trouble."

"It's no trouble," Katie assured her.

"And I insist on it," Rodney chimed in. "This whirlwind ceremony has obviously been stressful for you. With Katie's help, you'll have more time to relax."

Darla looked anything but relaxed by his idea. "That's asking too much of her. She's here as

Adam's guest. And isn't their date only supposed to last for the weekend?''

"That's the best part," Rodney said. "She and Adam can spend a few more days together. I know Adam will be thrilled." He turned to Katie. "And we'll compensate you for your work, so you won't have to worry about any lost wages.''

"Rodney, I..." Darla began.

But Rodney silenced her with a kiss. "No arguments. I'm going to pamper you for the rest of our lives, so you might as well start getting used to it.''

Darla lowered her gaze to the satin coverlet. "Whatever you say, Tater. But Katie may not *want* to stay. I'm sure she's a very busy woman.''

Rodney patted her hand. "Don't worry, Muffin, it's all settled." He turned to Katie. "Right?''

Katie ignored Darla's pointed glare and smiled at him. "I couldn't think of anywhere else I'd rather be.''

KATIE BEGAN to regret her words less than an hour later. More guests arrived, loaded with gifts and luggage. With Darla ensconced upstairs in her bed, Katie found herself in charge of making them welcome. When the arrivals became chaotic, Adam rode off on a white horse, and Rodney secreted himself away with his frail fiancée. But not before requesting Katie bake up a batch of Darla's favorite blueberry muffins for tomorrow's breakfast.

Her head began to ache at six o'clock. By ten o'clock it was throbbing. She couldn't put names with faces, but she did remember that the lady with blue hair demanded vegetarian fare during her stay.

And Darla's great-uncle, a dapper gentleman with a goatee, requested a spittoon in his room.

"There's no way I'm emptying that thing," Katie muttered to herself as she made her way outside for some fresh air.

Montana was breathtaking at night. Bright, twinkling stars filled the black velvet sky. In the distance she could see the faint ridges outlining the rugged mountain range. She breathed deeply, the pain in her head easing. Somewhere in the foothills, a lone coyote howled. She smiled as Wiley echoed his tinny howl in reply.

The stable door creaked when she opened it, and Wiley jumped and pawed at his pen, his claws scratching against the old wood.

"Hey there, Wiley," she said softly, entering his pen. He licked the tops of her shoes, then ran to his food dish. "Men," she muttered, feigning disgust as she pulled a handful of dog biscuits out of her pocket, "only think about one thing."

"Are we going to let her talk about us that way, Wiley?" intoned a low voice from the shadows.

Katie didn't turn. "And then there are those men that sneak up on a woman without any warning. You'd never do that, would you, Wiley?" The coyote pup was too busy gnawing on a dog biscuit to respond.

Adam moved up beside the open gate. "Sneaking is something coyotes do best."

"Some men I know are pretty good at it, too."

"I just came to tell you another guest has arrived."

Katie groaned. "Another one?" For a small, private ceremony, they'd certainly sent out enough wedding invitations. "Tell this one he'll have to bunk with Wiley."

"This one is Harvard Dunn, Lorene Baker's law partner. He probably uses a lot of the same tactics as a coyote in his law practice, but I doubt he'll sleep with one."

She brushed her hands together. "I suppose I need to find a bed for him somewhere. I wonder if he'd mind sharing a room with a spittoon."

"Hold it." Adam gently grasped her by both arms. "Dunn can find his own way around the house. You've done enough for one day."

His hands moved to her shoulders, gently massaging them. Katie swallowed her moan of pleasure. "That feels wonderful. Don't tell me—massage class was required at Lost Springs, too."

"Sarcasm makes my hands tired," he warned.

"Then I won't say another word." She closed her eyes as his hands worked her sore muscles. He must have decided she wasn't a threat to his company, after all. Or else he wanted to relax her into confessing everything. *It just might work.*

Adam moved closer to her as his fingers stroked the back of her neck. Her head lolled at the exquisite sensation.

"Feel good?"

"Mmm." She leaned against his broad chest. "I am now mush."

"I like mush." His lips skimmed along her jawline. "Although you taste more like blueberries."

Katie's eyes flew open. "The blueberry muffins! I forgot all about them."

"Relax," he murmured. "I took them out of the oven when the smoke alarm went off."

She winced. "Are they ruined?"

"Let's just say Wiley will have plenty to chew on during his teething period."

She pulled back, giving him the once-over. "Why are you being so nice to me?"

Amusement flashed in his blue eyes, and his hands dropped to her waist. He drew her closer to him. "Because men only want one thing."

"Why didn't you say so?" she said huskily. Then she reached into her pocket and pulled out a dog biscuit. "I have one left."

He laughed as Wiley began growling low in his throat, his black eyes trained on the biscuit. "Looks like he wants to fight me for it." He took the biscuit from Katie's hand.

Wiley responded by baring his teeth, his growls growing louder. The fur on the back of his neck stood up as his body tensed.

"Wiley, stop it," Katie scolded. "You've already had three."

"It's a coyote's natural instinct to fight for food." Adam dropped the dog biscuit on the pen floor, and Wiley pounced on it.

Katie bent down to ruffle his soft fur. "This coyote is going to learn some manners."

Adam didn't say anything for a long moment. Then he knelt next to her. "If we don't turn him back to the wild soon, he'll forget how to survive."

Katie edged closer to the pup. "I'll take care of him. He'll have enough dog biscuits to last him the rest of his life."

"You're not seriously thinking about keeping him?" Adam asked, the surprise evident in his voice.

"No, I'm not thinking about it. I've already decided."

Adam picked up one of Wiley's paws. The pup was too engrossed in his dog biscuit to even notice. "Look at the size of this paw. That's an indication of how big Wiley will be as an adult."

"Well, right now he's just a helpless puppy," she said, scratching Wiley's favorite spot behind his ear.

"I know he's cute." Adam reached out to scratch behind his other ear. Wiley's eyes closed in bliss. "But he's a predator, Katie, not a pet. He belongs in the wild."

"He belongs with me," Katie said stubbornly. Maybe she was being selfish. All she knew was that Wiley was all alone in the world, just like her. It made sense for the two of them to stick together.

But Adam wouldn't let it rest. "What will you do with him while you're waitressing? Chain him up behind the Roadkill Grill?"

"I haven't worked out all the details yet." She didn't tell him she had no plans to return to Lightning Creek. She wouldn't find her future there. The only problem was, where would she go? Especially with a coyote in tow.

Katie stood up. "Look, I don't want to talk about this anymore." She'd been too busy the last few hours to dwell on her problems. Now they all came rushing back. She didn't know her past and she didn't know her future. Rodney didn't recognize her, and Darla wasn't talking.

And then there was Adam. A man she'd known for only a few days. He made her laugh and made her feel like an attractive, desirable woman. He made her realize how very empty her life was. She couldn't handle him on top of everything else.

"I'd better go make another batch of blueberry muffins," she said, backing out of the barn.

Adam rose to his feet. "Katie, wait."

But she was already out the door. In two days the wedding would be over and she'd be on her own. Just like before.

It was time to get used to being alone again.

CHAPTER NINE

THE NEXT MORNING, Rodney requested a meeting with Adam and Katie in his library. Katie entered the room to find Adam the only one there. He leaned against a bookshelf, his arms folded. He looked comfortable and relaxed in a pair of tan Dockers and a white polo shirt. His gaze followed her as she walked into the room and sat in a brown Moroccan leather wing chair. She swallowed, all too aware of the sizzle of attraction between them whenever they were alone.

"He knows, doesn't he?" Katie said at last.

Adam arched a dark brow. "Knows what?"

She took a deep breath. "Rodney knows I broke into his office. He's going to ask me to leave."

Adam pushed off the bookshelf, moving toward her. He sat in the matching wing chair, leaning forward with his forearms resting on his knees. She couldn't help but notice his hands. The long, broad fingers. Those same fingers had meticulously molded a ceramic pot, tenderly bandaged an injured Wiley, massaged her neck and shoulders. A tingle shot through her at the remembered sensation.

"The last thing Rodney wants you to do is leave," Adam said, drawing her attention away from his hands. "You're becoming indispensable."

But Katie wasn't convinced. "Maybe he had another surveillance camera hidden in his office."

Adam shook his head. "There is only one security camera. And by the way, just in case you go in search of another pencil, the camera has been reactivated. There are too many people in this house to leave that room unsecured."

She nodded, wondering what other possible reason Rodney could have for calling this meeting. *Unless Darla had told him about her.* But told him what? That Katie had to leave because she made her dizzy? Darla still hadn't emerged from her suite.

Rodney breezed into the room, shutting the door behind him. "Where did all these people come from? This is supposed to be a small, intimate wedding."

"That reminds me," Adam said. "Darla's third cousin called from Butte and needs a ride out here."

Rodney sighed. "Darla has a big extended family. It's one of the things I love about her. But I'm drawing the line at third cousins. I'll put them up in a motel in Butte." He sat at the antique library table, waving away the subject as if it were a pesky fly. "Now we've got more important things to discuss." He turned to Adam. "Are you ready to give me the name of that thief you found in my office?"

Katie's gaze flew to Adam as her stomach twisted into a tight knot.

Adam leaned back in his chair. "I'm still conducting the investigation. But I don't think you have a leak on your hands. Right now all you need to worry about is your wedding."

Rodney tented his fingers under his chin. "That's the reason I wanted to meet with you both this morning. I've got a problem with the wedding. A big problem.''

Katie settled back in her chair. Wedding problems she could handle. It was all the other problems in her life that gave her trouble. ''What is it?''

''The vows.'' Rodney pushed up his glasses. ''Darla really wants us to write our own wedding vows.'' He looked at Adam, the panic plain on his face. ''You know I'm no good at that creative stuff.''

Adam stretched his long legs out in front of him. ''I know that's what you always claimed. Maybe if you hadn't paid someone else to write all your papers, you'd learn to like it.''

Rodney frowned. ''I had to pay for it after you quit writing them for free. Besides, this isn't like a term paper. I only need a few romantic lines to melt Darla's heart.''

Adam shrugged.

''Why don't you just stick with the classic love, honor and cherish, and Darla can promise to love, honor and obey?''

''Obey?'' Katie echoed. ''You're kidding, right?''

Adam looked at her, his brow furrowed. ''What's wrong with obey?''

Katie laughed. ''Spoken like a man. Why doesn't Rodney promise to obey?''

''Because it goes against tradition,'' Adam said, his tone even. ''The word *obey* has been in wedding vows for centuries. Why mess with a good thing?''

''Good for who?'' Katie challenged. ''Some egotistical male with a superiority complex? Let's come up with some vows that express love and mutual respect instead of male domination.''

Rodney stood up, a smile playing on his lips. ''Sounds like you two have it all under control. If you'll excuse me, I need to check on my fiancée.''

''You're missing my point,'' Adam said, after Rodney had left the room.

''No, I'm not,'' Katie countered. ''You believe a woman should let her husband tell her what to do. I believe a couple should communicate and solve their problems together.''

''Communicate?'' He folded his arms. ''Like when you stowed away in the back of my car without telling me? Or assaulted me with a phone instead of asking a simple 'Who is it?' ''

''In the first place, those are two completely different situations.'' Katie brushed a stray curl behind her ear. ''I had to hide in your car because you wouldn't listen to reason. Men are often unreasonable, which is why any woman would be nuts to obey one.''

He arched a brow. ''And just when did you become such an expert on husbands and wives?''

Her gaze flicked to the silver filigree wedding ring weighing heavily on her right hand, then up again. ''At the Roadkill Grill. You'd be amazed at what couples will discuss within hearing range of a waitress. It's like we're invisible.''

''I can't imagine you ever being invisible.''

Her cheeks warmed. ''Well, I can assure you I've been within hearing range of enough matrimonial battles to know men can be unreasonable.'' She tilted up her chin. ''You're a perfect example.''

"Me? I've been nothing but reasonable since the moment we met."

She looked at him in amazement. "You dumped me in a field of sagebrush and left me there!"

"Okay, so maybe one time—"

"You wanted to dump Wiley off on death row."

"Now that's not fair—"

Katie didn't give him a chance to defend himself. "And you accused me of trying to seduce your best friend."

"I never used the word *seduce*. See, this is a perfect example of how women communicate. They take what a man says and twist it around until he can't remember the perfectly reasonable words he said the first time."

"Look, this isn't getting us anywhere." She picked up a legal pad and two pens off the library table. "Why don't we each write our own version of an appropriate wedding vow, and Rodney can pick which one he likes best."

"Sounds good to me," Adam said as she tore off a piece of paper and handed it to him, along with one of the pens. "And just a word of warning—I used to get As on all my composition papers."

"Darla isn't going to grade Rodney, she's going to marry him. And I know what women like to hear."

"So do I. At least according to all the women in my past."

Katie made a show of looking around the room. "And where are they now? Probably with some man who doesn't have the word *obey* in his vocabulary."

He flashed her a grin. "Lucky for you."

With a sigh of exasperation, she bent over the

notepad. She stared at the blank piece of paper in front of her. For all her self-righteous debate, she didn't know how to begin to compose a heart-melting wedding vow.

She gazed at the ring on her finger. Had she used the standard vows at her wedding or composed her own? Had she married a man who had insisted on including the word *obey?* She squeezed her eyes shut, struggling to remember, but her mind wouldn't cooperate. The worst part was, whenever she thought of the word *husband,* she felt empty. If some man had dwelled in her heart in the past, he wasn't there now.

And whenever she thought of passion, she thought of...Adam.

"Done," he exclaimed, tossing his pen on the table as if this were a timed contest.

She couldn't help but smile at his exuberance. "Let me take a wild guess. You wrote, 'I, Rodney, take you, Darla, to be my obedient, wedded wife. I promise to love, honor and order you around from this day forward.'"

"Very funny." Adam leaned back in his chair. "If there's one thing I know how to do, it's romance a woman."

"All right," she challenged. "I'm Darla—romance me."

Katie's heart began to beat faster as he rose slowly to his feet. He moved toward her and held out his hand. Then he stood there and waited, his gaze never leaving her face. At last she lifted her hand until it touched his warm, broad fingers. He curled his hand around hers and pulled her easily to her feet.

"I, Rodney, take you, Darla," he said, stepping close to her, his hands tenderly cupping her face, "into my heart and into my life. To love and to honor. To adore and to cherish. For all my days and all my nights. I promise to give you all my love, all my loyalty and all of myself. Now and forever."

Then he kissed her.

A soft, gentle kiss full of promise and passion. When he finally lifted his head, Katie couldn't breathe.

The sound of applause from the open doorway startled her. She turned to see Rodney stride into the room, a wide smile on his face. "That was perfect."

Adam let go of her. "Glad you approve."

Katie stepped back, almost tripping over the chair. Her mouth still tingled from the feather-light touch of his lips. Adam sure knew how to make a woman melt.

"I definitely approve," Rodney said, looking from Adam to Katie. "In fact, I think we've discovered a hidden talent." He picked up the sheet of paper with the wedding vow on it. "Sure you two don't want to use this yourselves?" He grinned. "We could make it a double wedding."

"You're going to scare Katie away with that kind of talk," Adam said easily. "She bought a bachelor for the weekend, not forever."

Adam was right. She was scared. Because spending forever with Adam Harper didn't sound so bad. In fact, when he'd recited that vow, she'd almost believed him. Even worse, she wanted to believe him. Despite the fact she hardly knew him. Despite the number of times they'd clashed. Despite the wedding band on her finger.

Adam turned to Katie. "Now it's your turn."

She swallowed. "My turn?"

"To read the wedding vow you wrote. Then Rodney can declare the winner."

"I think it's unanimous," she replied, laughing as she held up her blank sheet of paper. "You win."

Adam scowled. "That hardly seems fair. I wouldn't have had to work so hard if I'd known there wasn't any competition."

"Hard work?" she scoffed. "You were done in less than a minute."

Rodney winked at her. "Someone must have inspired him."

"I am very impressed," she conceded. "You didn't use the word *obey* once." The last lines of his vow floated through her mind. *I promise to give you all my love, all my loyalty and all of myself. Now and forever.* For a brief moment, she wondered what it would be like to be on the receiving end of that kind of devotion.

Adam smiled. "I figured why bother since Tate is so infatuated with his wife-to-be that he'll probably let her walk all over him."

Rodney laughed. "My new motto is, 'What Darla wants, Darla gets.'"

"As long as you spelled it all out in black and white in the prenuptial," Adam replied.

"Oh, I didn't write a prenuptial."

Adam looked at him closely. "But your lawyer did, right?"

Rodney shook his head. "I don't want lawyers and their ten-dollar words to come between us. This is true love."

Adam sighed. "That's what you said about Candi.

And Fiona. And Estelle. And Kyla. If you'd married any one of them without a prenuptial, their divorce attorneys would have had a feeding frenzy."

Rodney grew mulish. "Darla's not like my other fiancées. She's different. And she's definitely not after my money."

"Then she won't mind signing a prenuptial agreement to prove it." Adam turned to Katie. "That's perfectly reasonable, isn't it?"

"It's reasonable," Katie said slowly, "but it's not very romantic."

"Exactly my point," Rodney exclaimed as he folded the wedding vow and placed it in his shirt pocket. "Hey, I almost forgot." He pulled a pink slip of paper out of the same pocket and handed it to Adam. "My secretary took a phone message for you."

"Thanks." Adam headed toward the door. "If I were you, I'd rethink that prenuptial agreement, Tate," he called over his shoulder on his way out.

Rodney's face grew pensive. "What would you do, Katie? Would you marry Adam if he demanded a prenuptial agreement?"

"I don't know," Katie replied softly. "I just don't know."

"CORINNE, this is Harper." Adam cradled the telephone receiver against his ear as he reached out to close the door to his bedroom. He wanted privacy for this conversation.

"Sorry it took so long to get back to you," Corinne began, "I tried to reach you yesterday afternoon, but you weren't in."

That's because he'd spent the day on horseback,

trying to keep away from Katie. Judging by his re-action to her in the stable last night, it hadn't worked. "No problem. What have you got for me?"

"Adam, you're not going to believe this."

He sank down on the bed, almost afraid to hear her report. "Try me."

"There is no Katie O'Hara."

His grip tightened on the telephone receiver. "Say that again."

"It's true," Corinne insisted. "There is no Katie O'Hara. She showed up in Lightning Creek about two months ago. But before that...nothing. I can't find any trace of her." Corinne Sullivan was one of his best employees. A fifty-seven-year-old widow with a sharp mind and an extensive investigative background, she'd worked vice in the Chicago Police Department for twenty years before hanging up her badge.

"There must be some mistake."

"Well, I've only been on it for twenty-four hours. I'm still following a couple of leads."

"What kind of leads?"

"I talked to your doorman again. He remembered another detail about the redhead who tried to con her way into your apartment. Apparently, she was wearing a wedding ring."

Adam's spirits lifted. Katie didn't wear a wedding ring. "How did he happen to notice that?"

"That's the first thing he checks when he sees a foxy babe. Those are his words, not mine."

Adam cracked a smile. "And your other lead?"

"A psychic we used to use down at the depart-ment has agreed to come to ExecTec and attempt a reading on this woman."

"Tell me you're joking."

"Hey, I'm desperate here, Adam." A long sigh carried over the line. "This one's really got me stumped. What exactly do you know about this O'Hara woman?"

What did he know about her? Only that her dark brown eyes drew him like a magnet. Her laughter left him wanting more. He knew she stirred something inside him, even when she wore a hairnet and a stained apron. *And the way she kissed.* He closed his eyes. Katie O'Hara made him feel things he didn't want to feel.

But he really didn't know her at all.

"Not much," he replied gruffly. "So what's your take on it?"

He could hear Corinne tapping a pencil on her front teeth. She always did that when a case disturbed her. "Corporate espionage?" she said at last.

"Katie's not the type."

"Well, then you have to consider the extremes. She could be a fugitive, hiding out in the middle of Wyoming. An escaped convict. Hell, she could even be in the Witness Protection Program. How else do you explain a woman with no past?"

Adam raked his hand through his hair. None of those explanations fit. "Look, she didn't just appear in Lightning Creek out of thin air."

"Actually, she came by ambulance," Corinne replied. "She was involved in a one-car accident on Shoshone Highway. Not far from that Lost Boys ranch."

"Lost Springs," Adam clarified. "How badly was she hurt?"

"Converse County Hospital won't release her records, of course. But according to the billing department she was there for over two weeks. So she must have been pretty banged up.''

''What about the cause of the accident?'' Adam asked, completely confident in Corinne's thoroughness.

''Still under investigation.''

That got his attention. ''But it happened over two months ago. How could the case still be open?''

''Good question. According to a Sheriff Hatcher, he's still missing a few vital details.''

''Details? What kind of details?''

''He declined to answer that question.''

Adam remembered a few run-ins with Sheriff Hatcher from his youth. The man could be implacable when it served his purposes. ''When was the date of the accident?''

He could hear the sound of papers being shuffled over the line.

''April tenth. The emergency call came in at 3:35 p.m.''

''Who reported it?''

''A local man. Name is Sam Duncan.''

Sam had found her? It made sense, actually. Not too many people had any reason to travel the highway between Lost Springs and Lightning Creek. So what was Katie doing there?

''What about the car?'' Adam asked. ''There should have been a name and address on the registration.''

''The car was totaled, most of the contents burned. Miss O'Hara either crawled out or was thrown from it after the accident.''

''What about the license plate number?''

"No license plate." The teeth tapping began again. "It was a brand new model and hadn't been registered or licensed yet."

Adam felt an odd sense of relief. "Well, if she was driving a new car we know she isn't a fugitive or an escaped con."

"Unless she stole the car," came the voice of reason on the other end.

"She's not that kind of woman," he said, knowing he sounded defensive.

"Well, I don't know the woman," Corinne conceded, "but she sounds like trouble to me."

"That's an understatement." She'd been nothing but trouble since he'd asked her to marry him in that barbecue line. That day he'd seen an attractive, sassy woman with barbecue sauce on her nose. Not a woman keeping secrets.

"So now what do you want me to do?"

"Keep digging," he replied.

"I don't think you understand. There's nothing to dig. I've reached rock bottom." More tapping. "Unless I can get Sheriff Hatcher to open up."

"Keep working on him," Adam replied. "If anyone can do it, you can."

She laughed. "Thanks for the vote of confidence, boss. Now, will you take a little advice?"

"I'm listening."

"Be careful, Adam."

A tight, hard knot formed in his chest. "One thing I do know. Whoever Katie O'Hara is, she's not dangerous."

Corinne didn't say anything for a long moment. "There are different kinds of danger."

"I'll keep my eyes wide open," he assured her

before hanging up. He absently rubbed the gnawing ache in his chest. *Damn.* He hated this. Hated the lies. The deception. The secrets.

He stalked out of his bedroom and down the long hallway, not giving himself time to rein in his temper. He flung open the door to her suite. But instead of confronting Katie, he found himself staring into an empty sitting room. No lights shone in the bedroom beyond, either. His rage dissolved as he took several long, deep breaths.

Maybe he was overreacting. Why should he expect her to confide her secrets to him? They barely knew each other. But all these unanswered questions bothered him. Unfortunately, a confrontation didn't guarantee any answers. He had other avenues to pursue before he started hurling accusations. He walked into the hallway, closing the door behind him.

Time. He just needed a little time. Then he'd have all the answers he wanted. The ache in his chest eased a little. Adam headed purposefully toward the stairway, a plan already forming in his mind.

Then he turned the corner and ran smack into Katie.

KATIE LAY sprawled on the carpet, slightly shaken from her collision with two hundred plus pounds of fast-moving male. Her head throbbed from the impact with the drywall. If this were a movie, her memory would come rushing back. She closed her eyes, waiting for the miracle to occur.

Adam swore under his breath.

"Are you all right?" His hands lightly skimmed over her body, obviously checking for compound fractures or protruding bones.

"I may have a slight concussion," she quipped, lying flat on the carpet. *And terminal amnesia.* No miracle for Katie. Why did she always have to do everything the hard way?

He leaned over her, gazing into her eyes. "Do you want me to call a doctor?"

"I think I'll live," she sighed, looking into his face. "You really do have beautiful eyes."

He sat back on his heels. "I think you're delirious."

"I'm fine." She sat up to prove it to him. Her head swam for a moment, so she blinked to clear it, then touched her fingertips to her temple. To her surprise, a small bump had formed.

"You are hurt," Adam muttered, trailing his fingers over the same bump.

"I think I hit the wall when you plowed into me. But I'm fine. Really." She stared at him. "Why were you in such a hurry, anyway?"

He dropped his fingers from her forehead. "No reason."

For a man who valued honesty, his words had a distinctly dishonest ring to them. She glanced down the hallway. The only rooms in this part of the wing belonged to her and the blue-haired vegetarian. "Were you looking for me?"

"Yes." He stood up. "I mean no."

"Which is it?"

He slowly backed away from her, moving toward the stairway. "It's yes. I want to talk to you. But not now. Later. Definitely later."

Now who sounded delirious? "Well, I'll be right here."

He stopped, an anxious expression on his face. "Are you sure you're all right?"

She smiled. "Positive. A little head trauma doesn't stop Katie O'Hara."

But he didn't look convinced. He took a couple of steps toward her. "Maybe I should carry you to your room."

Katie scampered to her feet before she gave in to the almost overwhelming temptation to let him do just that. Unfortunately, she had no trouble remembering the last time he'd carried her in his arms. The sinewy strength of his body. The sensation of his arms around her. The regret that had coursed through her when he let her go. Especially since she'd landed on a cocklebur.

"Thanks," she said, backing toward her bedroom, "but I can make it on my own just fine." They watched each other warily retreat. When Katie reached her room, she closed the door swiftly behind her. Then she leaned her back against it and slowly slid to the floor.

How had she ever gotten into this mess?

She was falling for him. Falling hard and fast for a man she barely knew. Although she knew him better than she knew herself. And that was the problem. She couldn't let herself be distracted by matters of the heart. Especially when there was a very good chance her heart belonged to someone else.

And even if it didn't, she couldn't let her guard down. Just two months ago someone had shot out the tires on her car. The doctors had told her repeatedly that it was a miracle she'd survived the accident. She couldn't count on another miracle to protect her. Until she knew who had tried to kill her and why, she couldn't trust anyone but herself.

Katie slowly rose to her feet. For now, Adam Harper could be nothing more to her than a weekend fantasy. And it was up to her to keep it that way. She walked into the bedroom and flipped on the overhead light.

That's when she saw it.

Katie's hand flew to her throat at the sight of the magenta letters streaked across her mirror. For a moment she couldn't breathe. She sagged to the bed, dropped her head between her knees and forced air into her lungs. At long last, she sat up and stared at the mirror.

The message was all too clear. *Keep your mouth shut, or else!* The words sent a chill through her. Or else what? She'd have another *accident?* Only she knew the first time wasn't an accident. Now someone was threatening her again. Someone in this house.

To Katie's surprise, she didn't fall completely apart. An icy calm descended on her. It was either shock or relief. Relief because she could finally face the nameless fear that had haunted her since she'd awoken in that bed at the Converse County Hospital.

She stood up and began to pace back and forth across the plush carpet. Rodney, Darla...even Adam. They were all connected with her past somehow. More than likely, it was one of them who'd left her the macabre warning on the mirror.

And which one of them had just come from the direction of her room, obviously in a hurry?

But she simply couldn't accept the most likely suspect. He might have had the means and the opportunity, but she knew in her heart Adam wouldn't resort to this type of cowardly behavior. He was too decent. Too noble. Too annoyingly honest.

So that left Rodney or Darla. She didn't have to have a fully functioning brain to know Darla wanted her long gone. And the lipstick-message-on-the-mirror trick seemed like just the kind of melodrama she would employ. Any woman who could turn a swoon into a two-day invalid act had melodrama in her blood.

Somehow, though, she couldn't see Darla staked out in a ditch on Shoshone Highway to shoot her car tires. The woman might be melodramatic but she was…nice. As much as Katie hated to admit it, she liked Darla. Rodney's fiancée had a fluffy innocence about her that Katie found endearing. Besides, anyone who could see Rodney's flaws and still want to marry him couldn't be all bad.

Or could she?

There was only one way to find out.

CHAPTER TEN

KATIE DIDN'T EVEN bother to knock. She flung open the door to Darla's suite and marched across the room, stopping at the foot of the canopy bed. "I know everything."

It was a bluff. A successful bluff, judging by the way the blood drained from Darla's face. For a moment, Katie thought the woman might faint again. But Darla recovered after a few moments, though her skin tone still matched the lacy white pillows propping her up in the bed.

"What do you want from me?" Darla whispered.

Katie plunked herself down on the corner of the bed. "I want the truth."

"You already know the truth."

Not exactly. But she didn't intend to show her hand. "I know my version of the truth. Now I'd like to hear yours."

Darla pressed her bloodless lips together.

"Of course, you don't have to say a word," Katie said, feigning a confidence she didn't feel. "That message on my mirror pretty much said it all."

Darla blanched. "You can't prove I wrote it."

Katie stifled a sigh of disappointment. She really hadn't wanted to believe Darla capable of such a threat. "Maybe I can't identify that unusual shade of lipstick.'' Katie let the words linger for a moment. ''But I bet Rodney can, or at least the handwriting.''

Darla shot straight up in bed. ''Please, Katie, you can't tell him. He wouldn't understand.''

''That his fiancée is making death threats? No, probably not. I don't understand it either, Darla. Would you mind explaining it to me?''

Darla sat mutely before her, a pout pursing her lips.

''Or would you rather explain it to the police?''

''All right.'' Darla relented bitterly. ''I'll tell you.'' She took a deep breath. ''The truth is I'm no better than Candi. Or Fiona. Or Estelle. Or Kyla.''

The names sounded vaguely familiar. ''Rodney's fiancées?''

''Ex-fiancées,'' Darla clarified, then her big blue eyes filled with tears. ''If you go to Rodney—'' she hiccuped through her tears ''—I'll be an ex, too.''

Against Katie's will, sympathy welled inside her. She reached over to pat Darla's hand. ''Just tell me everything. Maybe it can still work out.''

But Darla shook her head. ''No. It's too late. Rodney and I were going to be married…tomorrow…morning. And now…'' Darla flung herself sideways on the bed, sobbed hysterically into her pillow.

Katie waited for the tears to subside. And waited. And waited some more. After twenty minutes, she walked to the nightstand and picked up the pitcher of ice water. ''I'll give you five seconds to stop crying, or else I'm going to use drastic measures.''

Darla peered at her with red-rimmed eyes. She sniffed once. Twice. ''I'll stop.''

''Promise?''

Darla nodded. "It's just that I love Rodney so much. And now..." She hiccuped again, and her lower lip trembled ominously.

"You promised," Katie warned, eyeing the water pitcher.

Darla swallowed. "I should have known it was too good to be true. Nothing ever works out for me. Did you know I was crowned Miss Denver, but I was only halfway down the runway when they discovered an error in the vote tallies?"

"No, I didn't—"

"And in fourth grade, I had the star role in the school play, but I came down with the chicken pox on opening night."

"Gee, that's tough."

"Nothing ever turns out right for me," Darla exclaimed. "I broke my nose the night of the senior prom." She grabbed a tissue, dabbing at her eyes.

"You certainly can't tell it now," Katie said, trying to cheer her up.

"Plastic surgery," Darla said with a sniff. "My breasts are fake, too. Poor Rodney. Our entire relationship has been a lie."

Surely Katie's life hadn't been threatened over fake breasts. "Maybe now is the time to come clean. You can practice on me."

"But you already know everything. That's why you came here, isn't it? To get me out of the way."

Katie's mouth fell open. "What?"

Darla stuck out her chin, accusation glittering in her eyes. "I was right the first time. You want Rodney all to yourself."

"I don't want Rodney."

"Then why else are you here? And why—"

Darla's eyes narrowed, "—are you here under an assumed name?"

Katie's heart began to pound. "What makes you think Katie O'Hara isn't my real name?"

Darla snorted. "Oh, please. We both know you're Katrina Lansing, so you can stop playing games."

Katrina Lansing. It rolled off Darla's tongue so easily. Katie tried it. "Katrina Lansing," she murmured. The name seemed comfortable. Natural.

"Does Adam know your real name?" Darla asked.

"No."

Darla smoothed the coverlet. "So you're not in on this together?"

Katie made herself focus on Darla's words. "In on what?"

"A scheme to get Rodney's money."

Katie rolled her eyes. "I already told you. I don't want Rodney. Or his money."

"Then why are you trying to ruin everything for me?" Darla wailed. "Just because you're a hotshot investigator doesn't give you the right to meddle in other people's lives. You discovered all that money Rodney has coming to him, and now you want him for yourself."

An investigator. Katrina Lansing is an investigator. Katie sat on the bed. She couldn't quite grasp the fact that *she* was Katrina Lansing. *She* was a hotshot investigator. An investigator, not a waitress.

The dizziness returned, but this time it wasn't due to the bump on her head. She reached to the bedpost to steady herself. Like puzzle pieces firmly snapping into place, the memory of her name and career became clear. Now if she could just fit together the rest of the pieces of her life.

But first she had to make sense of Darla's weepy ramblings. "So you're saying that we're both gold diggers after Rodney's money, but you got to him first."

"I'm saying I *love* him," Darla insisted. "It may not have started out that way. Mother said it didn't matter."

"Mother?" Katie echoed as another puzzle piece snapped into place. Lorene Baker, senior partner at Baker and Dunn. *The law firm that had hired her three months ago.*

Darla looked past Katie's shoulder, her eyes widening with apprehension. "Mother."

Lorene Baker walked into the bedroom. "Yes, darling, Mother is here." She leaned over to kiss Darla's cheek, then turned to Katie. "My daughter seems overwrought. Perhaps we should let her rest." She motioned to the sitting room. "Would you join me in a cocktail, Ms. Lansing?"

Katie slowly rose, her knees shaky. As she followed Lorene into the sitting room, she could hear Darla dissolve into another bout of sobbing. A condescending smile flickered on Lorene's face as she closed the bedroom door behind her.

"Darla is a sensitive soul. So much like my former husband." She walked to the wet bar in the corner. "I, on the other hand, am a practical woman. Every problem has a solution, if you just look hard enough to find it."

Katie sank onto the sofa. She was so close to knowing everything. "Am I a problem?"

"I didn't think so," Lorene said evenly as she poured two drinks, "until now."

A prickle of unease lifted the hairs on Katie's neck. "Why now?"

Lorene handed her a snifter of brandy. "I think we both know the answer to that."

Katie wanted to scream. She didn't know the answer. She didn't know anything other than her name and occupation. But Lorene obviously did. Forcing herself to remain calm, she took a sip of brandy. *Play along,* she told herself. *Just be patient a little while longer.*

Lorene sat in the chair across from her. "As I said, I'm a practical woman. However, it's been my experience that most women tend to be...impractical. Take you, for instance."

Katie swirled the brandy in her glass. "How exactly am I impractical?"

Lorene smiled. "You gave up a wonderful job because of a man."

Katie's breathing hitched. A man. A husband? She held her breath, waiting for a revelation she didn't want to hear.

"And for what?" Lorene continued. "You left your position as lead investigator for one of the most prestigious law firms in Texas because you broke up with your fiancé, who happened to be one of the associates."

"Simon," Katie breathed. She *remembered* him. Tall, blond, with penetrating green eyes. They'd bickered a lot. He'd called it debate. Had she really been in love with him? Katie closed her eyes, searching her heart. But the only emotion she experienced when she thought of Simon was... disappointment.

"I don't remember his name," Lorene said, waving her hand in dismissal. "My point is, only a woman would let her emotions interfere with her career."

Katie swallowed. "Maybe I just needed a change. A new start."

Lorene leaned back in her chair. "Which Baker and Dunn gave you. I just wish you'd been a little more...appreciative."

Another wave of dizziness hit her. She took a sip of brandy, letting the smooth, bracing liquid wash down her throat. "I was searching for..."

"The lost Devlin heir," Lorene finished for her. "I'll admit you're very good. It only took you a few short weeks to find Rodney."

Katie slowly nodded. The Devlin heir. That's why Rodney's picture had seemed so familiar to her in Lightning Creek. She'd spent so much time studying it in her search. The search that had ended with that car accident.

The Devlin estate was worth millions of dollars. She'd been hoping to secure records at the Lost Springs Ranch for Boys that would verify her findings that Rodney Tate was the lost heir. The grandson of the rich and powerful Ox Devlin. Ox's estranged son had reportedly died, but rumors that he'd had a child before his death never did.

"The accident," she breathed, remembering how her search was abruptly halted.

"Accident?" Lorene echoed.

She swallowed. "I was involved in a car accident

two months ago, near Lost Springs. Someone shot out my tires.''

Lorene furrowed her brow. ''Are you saying it was deliberate?''

''The sheriff thinks so.''

Lorene shook her head, her lips compressed into a thin line. ''I knew those shirttail Devlin relatives were desperate to have the estate all to themselves, but I can't believe they'd resort to violence.''

Katie's head began to throb. ''How did they even know me? Or where to find me?''

''Obviously, they wanted to be kept informed of the search,'' Lorene replied. ''They claimed it was concern for their lost relative. But now I have to wonder.''

Katie frowned. ''Didn't you wonder why I had disappeared?''

Lorene shrugged. ''Not really. The case was solved. I assumed you were off on some personal female pursuit. Imagine my surprise when I saw you at the cocktail party.''

Katie looked at her, suddenly curious. ''Why didn't you approach me right away?''

''Well, we both know that is a matter of delicacy.''

Katie was still trying to process this sudden barrage of information. ''So that's why Darla fainted when she saw me.''

Lorene pursed her lips. ''As I said, she's a sensitive girl. Darla recognized you from the picture in your résumé. She did some office work for the firm over her Christmas break, shortly before our first telephone interview.''

''And your partner, Mr. Dunn?'' she asked, remembering the balding, slightly pompous attorney. He hadn't given her a second glance.

"Harvard has just returned from an extended stay in Europe. As I said during your job interview, he's really more of a figurehead at Baker and Dunn." Lorene set down her glass. "Now, may I ask you a question?"

Katie nodded, still trying to fit all the pieces together in her mind.

"Why are you here under an assumed name?"

"It's a long story."

"And an interesting one, I am sure. But for now, we must be practical and deal with the matter at hand." Lorene pulled a checkbook out of her purse. "How much?"

Katie blinked at her in surprise. "What?"

"Come now, Katrina, let's not play games. You have access to information which is potentially damaging to my daughter's happiness. I'm willing to pay you to keep your mouth shut."

"You want to *bribe* me?" But why? Katie wondered. What information was Lorene talking about?

"Bribe is such a distasteful word. Let's just say I want to finance your continued silence on a certain subject."

Then it hit her. "Rodney doesn't know he's the Devlin heir."

"Not yet." She clicked the Mont Blanc pen in her hand. "Now, can we agree on an amount in the six-figure range?"

But Katie barely heard her. Her mind spun as more of the perplexing puzzle became clear to her. Rodney Tate, already a wealthy man, was heir to a multi-million-dollar fortune and didn't know it.

Darla did know it, and that's why she wanted to marry him. It was also the reason she suspected Katie wanted Rodney for herself. No wonder the woman had fainted. Katie O'Hara, or rather Katrina Lansing, was the only one who knew Lorene and Darla's dirty little fiscal secret.

Unfortunately, much of Katie's personal life still remained a blank. She knew about her failed engagement to Simon, but the rest of the past lay behind a mist in her mind. The shapes were there, but she couldn't quite make them out.

She stood up, her head throbbing, and made her way toward the door. "I'm not feeling well. I have to go."

"Certainly. We can negotiate the precise terms later." Lorene replaced the checkbook in her purse. "But just tell me one thing."

She turned. "Yes?"

"How much does Mr. Harper know?"

Adam. The implications of her returning memory washed over her in full force. She was free. No husband in her past. Just a self-absorbed ex-fiancé. She gazed at the wedding band on her finger, relief almost overwhelming her. *It was her grandmother's ring.* Her beloved grandmother, Katya, an immigrant from Czechoslovakia. She'd taught Katrina to knit and make kolaches.

Grandma Katya had died last year.

That's why the ring had given her comfort. Katie had worn it on her left hand after her breakup with Simon because she hadn't been able to handle the interest of other men at the time.

Now she looked forward to the interest of other

men. Or rather, one man in particular. She had to find Adam.

"I asked you a question, Katrina." Lorene's voice echoed behind Katie as she escaped from the suite. The pounding in her head matched her rapid footsteps. More isolated memories flashed in her mind. An image of herself in a ballet costume. A light blue Volkswagen bug. *Her first car.*

By the time Katie had checked Adam's room, the stables and the kitchen, his usual haunts, her desire to see him bordered on panic. "Get a grip, O'Hara," she murmured to herself. "I mean…Lansing. Get a grip, Lansing."

Part of her missed her alter ego already. She'd lived as Katie O'Hara for two months. Katrina Lansing was still too new to her. Too unfamiliar.

She stopped in front of Rodney's private office. The door was open, but only one man occupied the room.

"Hey, Katie, I'm glad you're here." Rodney walked across the room, a catalog in his hand. "Believe it or not, I still haven't gotten Darla a wedding gift." He shoved the catalog under her nose. "Do you think she'd prefer a pearl necklace or these diamond earrings?"

Katie closed her eyes for a moment to balance her equilibrium. "Where is Adam?"

Rodney chuckled. "Adam doesn't know a thing about jewelry. Besides, I need a woman's opinion."

Katie reluctantly glanced at the catalog. As heir to the Devlin estate, he could buy the entire inventory without blinking. "I'm sure she'll be happy with anything you give her."

"But I want it to be something special."

"Why?"

He frowned at her. "Because Darla is special, of course. She's beautiful, and sweet, and wonderful."

"What if you found out she wasn't so wonderful? What if you suddenly discovered some things about Darla that weren't…perfect?"

Rodney sighed. "Katie, I know why you're asking me this."

She blinked at him. "You do?"

He placed a consoling hand on her shoulder. "I know you're attracted to me, but it just isn't going to work out."

Katie stifled a groan, which Rodney misinterpreted. "I know it's hard to accept, but it's for the best. Darla is the only woman for me—for better or for worse."

That answered her question. She looked at him, torn by indecision. Did she tell him now? Before she had all the holes filled in her story? The marriage ceremony was scheduled for eleven o'clock tomorrow morning. That gave her less than twenty-four hours to sort everything out.

One word from her and the entire wedding would go up in flames. It was a lot of responsibility for a woman who had just learned her own name.

"May I make a suggestion?" Rodney asked gently.

"Of course."

"Forget about me. In fact, it might be best if you left."

Her mouth dropped open. "Left?"

He grasped her shoulders, gazing soulfully into her eyes. "Think about it. How will you feel watching me take Darla as my wife tomorrow?"

Good question. She wished she knew the answer. Could she let Rodney marry a woman he admittedly loved? A woman marrying him for all the wrong reasons. Yet Darla claimed she loved him. Katie shook her head, more confused than ever. "I can't leave."

"I know it won't be easy, but..."

"No," Katie said firmly, forestalling any argument. Between her confusion and her aching head, she didn't have the energy to set Rodney straight. "Where's Adam?"

Rodney dropped his hands from her shoulders. "He's gone."

She blinked at him. *"Gone? But that's impossible. I just ran into him a short while ago." Literally* ran into him. And she had a bump on her head to prove it.

"You don't mean he's gone for good, do you?"

Rodney looked at her. "I hope you're not planning to turn to Adam on the rebound."

She closed her eyes and counted to ten. "Please, Rodney, just tell me where he is and if he's coming back."

Rodney sighed. "He'll be back sometime this evening. He drove into Butte on business."

"He left without telling me?" Katie said aloud, more to herself than to Rodney.

"Don't take it personally. He seemed a little distracted."

"Yes, he did," she murmured, remembering the way he'd plowed into her. The only question was why. She reached up to touch her sore temple. She couldn't think clearly with her head pounding this way. She needed a bottle of industrial-strength aspirin and a nice, long nap. Maybe by the time she awoke, Adam would be back.

Then what? She could tell him her real name and her real occupation. Her real reason for coming to Montana with him. Then he'd know she'd been lying to him from the start. Lying to a man who hated deception of any kind.

She could finally tell Adam the truth. And lose him forever.

ADAM'S BUSINESS took him to the Red Eye Diner in downtown Butte. The heavy aroma of hot grease hit him as soon as he walked through the door. Honky-tonk music crackled through a stereo speaker duct-taped to the lunch counter. A chalkboard above the counter listed the daily special as chicken and dumplings. The diner catered to ranchers and truck drivers, and Adam knew from previous visits to Butte that it served the best food in town. He nodded at a waitress, then let his gaze wander around the room.

To his surprise, he saw Marge Olson seated at a back booth, eyeing a big slab of lemon meringue pie on a plate in front of her. He ambled over to her. "Marge, what are you doing here?"

She grinned. "Hey, there, Harper. You look almost as good as this pie."

He slid into the booth opposite her. "I hope Sam's around here somewhere. He was supposed to meet me here."

She nodded. "He's off buying a wedding present for that Tate fellow." Marge picked up her fork. "He sure was tickled to get a wedding invitation. And I was even more tickled when Sam allowed me to tag along with him to Montana."

"Are you his date for the wedding?"

Marge laughed. "Date? Not even close. My heart belongs to a slow-talking cowboy who works at a ranch outside of Butte. I'm here to surprise him."

Adam watched Marge fork up a big bite of pie, her eyes closing in ecstasy as she chewed. He glanced at his watch. "I need to talk to Sam about Katie. Will he be here soon?"

"Hard to tell. But since I know the girl better than anyone, you can talk to me." Marge winked at him. "Do you want to ask my permission for her hand in marriage?"

He leaned back against the bench. "Marriage? We only met four days ago."

She shrugged her bony shoulders. "Sounds like long enough to me. Either the sizzle is there or it isn't."

The sizzle was definitely there. He felt it every time he looked at her. And when they kissed... Adam tugged at his shirt collar. When they kissed that sizzle threatened to burn out of control. He cleared his throat. "A relationship needs more than sizzle," he said, trying to convince himself as much as Marge. "You can't just jump into it with your eyes closed or you might have to pay the consequences."

She snorted. "That's bunk. Look at this piece of pie." She pointed to it with her fork. "It looks so good it makes my mouth water. And I know it tastes good. So should I sit around worrying about the consequences if I eat it? Sure, it might put some more padding on my hips. Maybe even cause a cavity or two. But while I'm sitting here fretting about it, someone else could come along and take it away from me. Then they end up enjoying it and I end up with nothing."

"You could always order another piece of pie."

She shook her head. "I've already had a taste of this one. It's the best piece of pie around. Why should I have to settle for second best?"

He shook his head. "This is ridiculous. You can't compare the two. Besides, I don't want to talk about pie. I want to talk about Katie."

She scooped up a generous bite of meringue. "I thought we were talking about Katie."

Adam leaned forward. "All right. Then tell me everything you know about her."

She swallowed the meringue, then licked her fork. "Why?"

"Because...I have reason to believe she's not who she says she is."

Marge waved her fork at him. "That is exactly my point. While you worry over the small details, some other man could come along and sweep her off her feet."

"This isn't a small detail." He raked his fingers through his hair. "I don't even know if I can trust the woman."

"You can trust her." Marge took another bite of pie.

"How do you know that?" he asked impatiently. "She only showed up in Lightning Springs two months ago. Did you know her before then?"

"Nope," Marge replied, smacking her lips as she scraped the last crumbs off her plate. "Never set eyes on her before."

"Do you know where she came from? Any details about her family or her background?"

Marge shook her head, every hair of her black beehive firmly in place. "Katie didn't like to talk about her personal life. And I'm not one to pry."

"So what makes you think I can trust her?"

Marge pushed her plate away, then looked him straight in the eye. "Because I know people. I've been a waitress for the last forty years, and I've seen all kinds come and go. Take you, for instance."

Adam narrowed his eyes. "What about me?"

She leaned back against the padded red vinyl bench and pulled a pack of cigarettes out of her pocket. She tapped the pack against her hand and drew out a long, slim cigarette. "You're easygoing on the outside but locked up tight on the inside. You don't want anybody, especially a woman, to know your secrets."

"What makes you think I've got secrets?"

"Because everybody has secrets." Marge struck a match against the tabletop, then held it to the tip of her cigarette. She inhaled deeply before blowing a smoke ring in the air above her. "Even Katie. Maybe if you tell her yours," she said with a cackle of laughter, "she'll tell you hers."

Adam bit back a sigh of frustration. This wasn't getting him anywhere. He drummed his fingers on the table, wondering how much longer he should wait for Sam.

"So do you want me to tell you what I do know about Katie?" Marge asked.

Adam's hopes rose. "Yes. Tell me everything."

Marge tapped her cigarette ashes into the tin ashtray in the center of the table. "Katie O'Hara is fun, sweet, generous and lost."

He looked at her in surprise. "Lost?"

She sighed. "Yes. Katie O'Hara is a lost soul. I don't know how and I don't know why, but she's alone, Adam. And lonely."

"Doesn't she have any family? Any friends?"

Marge shrugged. "Who knows? She won't talk about her personal life, and I respect that. As I said before, we all have our secrets."

Only Katie had too many secrets. Before he could interrogate Marge further, a big hand slapped his shoulder. Adam looked up to see Sam Duncan's lined face split into a grin.

"Howdy, Harper." Sam extended his hand.

Adam stood and returned the older man's firm handshake. He'd seen him at the bachelor auction but only had time for a brief chat. Sam had aged over the years, but who wouldn't trying to corral three generations of wayward boys? "Hello, Sam. How are you?"

Sam slid into the booth next to Marge. "Well, I've got arthritis from bending so many of you boys over my knee."

Adam bit back a smile. Sam had never raised a hand to his boys. He'd had a much more effective punishment for his unruly charges—mucking out horse stalls. And he'd always seemed to save his long, drawn-out lectures until you were knee-deep in manure.

"Adam's been getting antsy waiting for you." Marge snubbed out her cigarette. "He wants to know all about Katie. He doesn't trust her."

"I never said that—" Adam began.

Sam's chuckle cut him off. "Now that's a coincidence. Last time I talked to Katie, she wasn't sure she could trust you."

Adam folded his arms across his chest. "I hope you set her straight."

"Sure did," Sam replied. "Just like I'm going to set you straight. Katie O'Hara is a fine woman and any man dumb enough not to trust her doesn't deserve her." He narrowed his eyes. "Are you that dumb, Harper?"

"No, sir." Adam smiled. Whether it was the stern tone of Sam's voice or the familiar echo of similar words from long ago, he could almost smell the pungent aroma of horse manure.

"Good. Now go back and lasso that girl before she gets away."

"It's not that simple." He looked at Sam. "You found her after that car accident?"

Sam nodded. "Sure did. She's lucky she survived."

"How did it happen?"

Sam shrugged. "I don't know for sure. The newspaper article was short on details. Looked to me like both her back tires blew out and her car went out of control. It skidded right past cottonwood Gully, then rolled twice." He looked at Adam. "You remember that spot?"

He remembered it, all right. A straight twenty-foot drop. Sam was right. Katie was lucky to be alive. His heart hammered at the thought of her in that kind of danger. "What was she doing on Shoshone Highway, anyway?"

Sam shrugged. "Never found out. Maybe she wanted to tour the ranch. Or maybe she was looking for a job. She did end up hiring on at the Roadkill Grill right after she got out of the hospital."

Adam clenched his jaw. "That doesn't tell me anything more than I already know."

Marge rolled her eyes. "What do you want? An FBI background check?"

"That might be a nice start."

Marge threw her hands up in the air. "I give up. There's no such thing as guarantees. Especially in romance. You've either got to take a chance and risk it all, or play it safe. And in my book, safe is for cowards."

"The Adam Harper I know is no coward," Sam intoned.

Maybe they were right. It was time to stop playing it safe.

CHAPTER ELEVEN

KATIE AWOKE SLOWLY from a deep, dreamless sleep. A full moon shone through her window. A glance at the clock on her bedstand told her it was just after midnight. She lay back on her goose-feather pillow, her eyes closed as she searched her memory.

It was no use.

Her past was still full of gaping holes. Her headache had disappeared, but no new memories had surfaced. She knew her name, her occupation and her marital status. She sighed as she pushed the bedclothes aside and climbed out of bed. Maybe that was enough for now.

She padded across the bedroom, pulled off her nightgown and slipped into her freshly laundered denim dress and leather sandals. The nap had refreshed her, even if it hadn't helped her come up with any more answers. She was wide awake and restless.

She walked noiselessly downstairs, the house unusually quiet. Everyone had retired early in anticipation of the big day tomorrow. A wedding she could stop simply by revealing the secret of the Devlin heir.

As she wandered onto the front porch, she considered Rodney's suggestion. She could leave tonight and forget about Rodney and Darla and those dangerous Devlins.

But could she forget about Adam?

She hugged herself as a cool mountain breeze drifted across the porch. She didn't want to think about Adam. For the first time in a long while, she *wanted* to forget. She skipped off the porch and headed for the stables. She could always count on Wiley to distract her. The crafty coyote pup was living up to his name, getting into all kinds of mischief. He'd chewed open several sacks of expensive horse feed and had made a habit of escaping from his pen.

She opened the stable door, surprised to find a light on inside. She was even more surprised when she saw Adam. He stood next to Wiley's pen, dressed in a blue chambray shirt, a pair of faded denim jeans and cowboy boots. The heavy growth of dark whiskers on his jaw made him look like an outlaw.

He'd already stolen her heart.

Her pulse quickened. For the first time she could let herself imagine the possibilities with this man. She could desire him without guilt. And desire him she did.

He turned to watch her as she walked slowly into the stable. ''Katie, there's something I need to tell you.''

''Yes, Adam?'' she said softly.

''Wiley is gone.''

''WHERE WOULD you go if you were a coyote?'' Katie asked as she and Adam walked the perimeter of the fence line. They'd been searching for over an hour, following Wiley's paw prints out of the yard and into the pasture, where they'd disappeared in the tall grass.

"The nearest coyote bar," Adam said, leaning against a weathered fence post, "for a cold beer and a dance with a pretty female coyote."

She frowned at him. "This is serious, Adam. Wiley is out there all alone somewhere."

"Listen," he said, drawing her close to him, her back pressed against his chest. "Just listen."

Katie closed her eyes as he wrapped his arms around her waist, his chin lightly resting on the top of her head. His large frame protected her from the cool breeze.

Then she heard it. The sound of raucous howls in the distance. Several coyotes joined in the chorus.

"Wiley's out there," Adam murmured next to her ear, "where he belongs. He's probably snuggling up to some pretty female coyote right now, showing her all his new tricks."

"Just what kind of tricks did you teach him?" she asked, her voice slightly shaky.

Adam's arms tightened around her. "I can't give away all my secrets. But I will tell you one. It might make you feel better." His deep voice rumbled in her ear, the vibrations sending a tingle through her.

"I'm not sure anything you tell me can make me feel better," she said, her voice breaking. "I miss him already."

"I know," he murmured, gently rocking her in his arms.

Her body gradually relaxed into his, relishing his strength and his warmth. "All right. Tell me your secret."

"When I was ten years old," Adam began, "our neighbor gave me a puppy. It was so ugly nobody else would take him. But I thought he was perfect. He had big floppy ears, enormous paws, and he liked to chew on everything."

A reluctant smile curved her mouth. "Sounds familiar."

"He was a lot like Wiley," Adam affirmed. "A furry ball of mischief. Even my stepfather liked him. Unfortunately, the man didn't like me."

She could feel his muscles tense and hear the way his voice hardened. "Your stepfather left you at Lost Springs."

Adam didn't say anything for a long moment. "It was his idea, though my mother agreed. But this story isn't about me, it's about Alfred."

Her smile widened. "You named him Alfred?"

He chuckled. "All right, so it's not your typical dog's name."

"How did you ever come up with Alfred?"

Adam hesitated. "It's a long story."

She leaned her head against his chest. "We've got all night. And I'd really like to know."

"It was my Dad's name. Alfred Harper."

She could hear the change in his voice, laced with both love and pain. Katie sucked her lower lip between her teeth, hurting for him.

Adam cleared his throat. "My dad was killed in a motorcycle accident when I was ten years old. My mother remarried only a few months later."

"Oh, Adam." She turned in his arms to face him. "I'm sorry."

He smiled. "Hey, this story is supposed to cheer you up. Now where was I?"

"You and your dog Alfred, making mischief."

"Oh, right." Adam reached out to tuck a stray curl behind her ear. "Anyway, Alfred was my best friend. We went everywhere together. Except Lost Springs."

She looked at him. "Please tell me this story has a happy ending."

"It does," he assured her, wrapping his hands around her waist. "Just let me finish."

"Sorry." Katie was suddenly aware of how close they stood together, face-to-face. His hard, lean body brushed against hers in so many places, setting off little sparks of pleasure inside her.

"When my folks dropped me off at Lost Springs," he continued, "my biggest worry was Alfred. I had no idea what would become of him. So of course, I imagined the worst."

Katie's imagination kicked in as Adam rubbed his hands in slow circles across her back. She imagined unbuttoning his chambray shirt and splaying her fingers over his warm, broad chest. She envisioned pressing her lips to his chest, then his neck and that delicious mouth. She closed her eyes, making herself focus on his words.

"I pictured him begging on the streets or sitting on death row in the dog pound."

She punched him playfully in the ribs. "That's where you wanted to put Wiley."

"But I didn't, did I?"

"No," she admitted grudgingly, "instead he's lost out here in the wilds of Montana."

"He's exactly where he wants to be," Adam reminded her. "Wiley's the one who found a way out of the stable, remember."

"I suppose you're right." She sighed. "So tell me what happened to Alfred."

"Well, when I couldn't stand it anymore, I went to see Sam Duncan."

"I know Sam," Katie said with a smile. "He comes in for coffee every morning at the Roadkill."

"I begged him to let Alfred come to Lost Springs. I promised to take care of him, do extra chores, even share my meals with him so they wouldn't have to spend money on dog food."

She held her breath. "What happened?"

Adam smiled. "Sam said yes. He believed boys and dogs belonged together. There were always three or four mutts running around the ranch, and Sam told me one more wouldn't matter. So I wrote a letter to my mother, asking her to send Alfred to me."

Katie's heart constricted. "And did she?"

He shook his head. "She never got the letter. She and my stepfather had moved to Canada by then."

She frowned at him. "Is this the happy part?"

He grinned. "I'm getting to it. A few months later I got a Christmas card in the mail."

"From your mother?"

"No, from Alfred."

Katie blinked at him. "Okay, now I'm really confused."

"It was a picture of my dog, wearing a red elf's hat and sitting in front of a Christmas tree. On the back of the picture was a note that read, Merry Christmas, Love, Alfred."

"So did he end up at the North Pole?"

Adam laughed. "No, my folks took him with them to Canada. He was fine. Just fat and happy and spoiled rotten. All that time I'd worried for nothing.''

Katie stared at him. This was the happy ending? His mother and stepfather took the dog and left their son behind. She didn't know whether to laugh or cry. So she did both. "Oh, Adam," she said, laughter mingling with her tears. "That's the saddest story I've ever heard.''

"Hey," he said, looking puzzled as he brushed a teardrop off her cheek, "I'm trying to make you feel better.''

She cried harder. "I know.''

He looked totally disconcerted by her tears. "The point of the story is that Alfred lived happily ever after. And so will Wiley.''

"I know," she said, wiping her tears away. "But I'm not so sure I will. Wiley is all I've got.''

Adam gazed into her eyes as he drew her closer to him. "No. He isn't.'' Then he kissed her.

It was a soft, healing kiss, his lips just grazing hers. Katie moaned softly when he lifted his head. Adam was right. It was time for her to let Wiley go. It was time to move on with her life, too. No more hiding from her future—whatever it may be. So she wrapped her arms around his neck and drew him down to her mouth once more.

He tangled his fingers in her hair as his mouth met hers. He deepened the kiss, and the heat of his passion dissolved any lingering doubts. He needed her as much as she needed him. And Katie wasn't going to deny either one of them any longer.

"The house," he rasped. "We should go to the house.''

"Here," she murmured against his lips, her fingers fumbling with the buttons on his shirt. She didn't want to break this spell between them. Didn't want to have time for second thoughts. She wanted him under the stars in this wide-open meadow. Here, where it seemed as if they were the only two people in the world. The soft grass was their bed and the moon their candlelight.

Adam groaned low in his throat when she released the last button of his shirt and pulled it out of his jeans. She kissed the hot pulse point at the base of his throat. Then she peeled the shirt over his broad shoulders. They both dropped to their knees on the silky grass, breathing hard as they gazed in wonderment at each other.

With a tentative hand she reached out to touch his broad, bare chest. His hard muscles flexed beneath her fingers as she smoothed them over a round, flat nipple to the washboard ripples of his stomach.

"Katie," Adam groaned, his eyes closed.

She continued her tender exploration, tracing one finger over a faint scar on his collarbone. He clenched his jaw as he kneeled motionless before her. Then he opened his eyes and reached for her.

She gasped softly as he took her mouth, molding it with his, teasing it open with his tongue. Then he laid her gently on the grass, hovering above her as his hand trailed over her cheek, down the column of her throat to the rounded bodice of her denim dress. She closed her eyes as he traced the trail with his mouth.

A chorus of night sounds surrounded them. Moonlight reflected the desire in his blue eyes as he slowly removed her dress. "You are so beautiful."

The cool night air washed over Katie's naked

body, and she shivered with anticipation. He moved over her, his hot, bare skin warming her, arousing her passion.

And her conscience.

"Adam," she gasped, her body arching beneath him as he worshipped her breasts with his mouth. "Wait."

He trailed kisses up her throat, capturing her mouth once more. "I want you, Katie. I…need you."

She moaned at the raw emotion in his voice. "But you don't really know me. I'm not…the woman you think I am."

"I know everything I want to know," he murmured against her mouth. "I love everything about you. The way you talk and move and taste. I love…you."

He swallowed her response with his mouth, almost as if he was afraid to hear it. His hands never stopped touching her, caressing her with heated intent. His lips coaxed and teased and beguiled until she couldn't think about anything but touching him. Making him experience the same dizzying heights of pleasure.

She wrapped her arms around him as he entered her, relishing the weight of his body and his low rumble of satisfaction. Closing her eyes, she willed herself to forget everything.

Everything except this incredible moment in time.

ADAM AWOKE slowly, wincing at the bright sunlight streaming through the windows. He blinked, disoriented for a moment by the white lace coverlet draped over him. Then a soft, warm body nestled against him, and the heated memories of last night came rushing back.

They'd made love in the meadow—twice—then somehow found enough strength to return to the house. He grinned, remembering Katie's surprise when they'd found Wiley, safe and sound, asleep in his pen. And how they'd celebrated by making love in the hayloft.

They'd barely made it to Katie's bedroom before losing themselves in each other once more.

He gazed at her face, so relaxed and peaceful in sleep. He tenderly pulled a blade of hay from her auburn curls. Adam caressed her hair, then the creamy, smooth skin of her bare shoulder. He wanted her all over again.

Katie turned toward him, a soft sigh of satisfaction leaving her parted lips. He lightly kissed her succulent mouth, then forced himself to climb out of bed. If he didn't leave now, he might never leave. As tempted as he was to love her all over again, Rodney might not appreciate his best man skipping the wedding.

He watched Katie sleep as he silently slipped into his clothes. He loved her. Even more amazing, he'd told her he loved her. Adam Harper had never said those words to a woman before. He whistled as he made his way downstairs to the kitchen, where he discovered Rodney in the breakfast nook.

"There's a hot breakfast buffet in the dining room," Rodney said as he spread cream cheese on a bagel. "If you don't mind standing in line."

"This looks good to me," Adam replied, grabbing a blueberry muffin out of the basket on the table. "How is the bridegroom this morning?"

"I'm great. You look pretty cheerful yourself."

"Why not? It's a beautiful day and love is in the air."

Rodney put down his bagel. "Then I hope what I'm about to tell you won't dampen your mood."

"Impossible," Adam said, helping himself to a glass of grape juice.

Rodney picked at his bagel. "Look, I would have told you this last night, but you got back from Butte too late." He hesitated. "I've asked Katie to leave."

Adam lowered his juice glass. "Please tell me you're joking."

"No, I'm not joking. I really think it would be best."

"You've just spent the last few days trying to throw us together."

Rodney averted his gaze, staring intently at the toaster. "That was before..."

An ominous gnawing began in Adam's gut. He almost knew he didn't want to hear this. But he'd never been a coward and he wasn't about to start now. "Before what?"

"Before she came on to me."

Adam's tension eased. "We've been through this before. If a woman asks if you'd like cream in your coffee, you think it's a come-on."

The color rose in Rodney's cheeks. "That was before I met Darla. I'm not as insecure about women as I used to be. And she did kiss me."

"Who, Darla?"

Rodney rolled her eyes. "No...I mean, yes. Of course, Darla kisses me. But so did Katie."

Adam's gut tightened. "So let me get this

straight. I bring a date with me to your wedding, and you make a move on her?''

"She's the one who came to my bedroom.''

"I don't believe you.''

Rodney set his jaw. "Maybe not. But I'm telling you the truth. I've been a jerk lately, and this is the only way I know how to make it up to you.''

"By seducing my date?''

"I didn't touch her,'' Rodney declared, then shrugged as he leaned back in his chair. "Well, all right, I did kiss her back. I had a case of cold feet and wanted to convince myself that I wasn't making a big mistake.''

Adam curled his fist around his glass, wishing it was Rodney's scrawny neck. "I'd say you did make a big mistake. If you ever touch her again…''

Rodney held up one hand. "No problem. I know now that Darla is the only girl for me. Only…''

"What?'' Adam bit out the question. He was tired of Rodney's games. The half-truths and embellished stories he'd spun since childhood. He closed his eyes, remembering the way Katie's mouth had clung to his last night. The way her soft, enticing body had curled around him.

Rodney leaned forward. "The truth is, Katie approached me again yesterday. She tried to talk me out of marrying Darla.''

"Why the hell would she do that?''

Rodney sighed. "I suppose for the usual reason.''

Adam snorted. "Your money? You think she's another gold digger?'' He wouldn't let himself admit he'd thought the same thing at one time.

"I should recognize one by now, don't you think? It only took me four ex-fiancées to figure it out. Besides, it's not like my fantastic good looks are drawing all these women to me."

"Well, Katie isn't one of them."

Rodney arched a skeptical brow. "How can you be so sure?"

"Because I know her." As soon as he said the words, her voice echoed in his mind. *You don't really know me. I'm not the woman you think I am.* He steeled himself as the first insidious doubts sprouted inside him.

"You only met her a few days ago," Rodney countered. "Face it, Adam, you don't know anything about Katie O'Hara. The truth is, she came on to me. And just yesterday, she bad-mouthed Darla, insinuating she wasn't the right woman for me."

"Katie would never bad-mouth anyone."

"Okay, so she put it more politely than that. She still tried to drive a wedge between me and my bride-to-be. And when I *politely* asked her to leave, she refused."

Adam didn't want to listen anymore. Didn't want to wonder why she'd never said a word to him about it last night. She was worried about Wiley, he told himself. Too worried to think about anything else. And later they'd been too wrapped up in each other for conversation.

"Look, Adam," Rodney said, his voice low. "I don't have any ulterior motives here. As your friend, I'm just trying to look out for your best interests."

"So why do I have so much trouble believing that?" Adam replied, letting the sarcasm drip from his voice. "Could it be because you've gone after every other woman I've ever dated?"

"Only after you broke up with them," Rodney

clarified. "Besides, Katie came to me. I just thought I should warn you."

Adam snorted. "Well, in the future, don't do me any more favors."

But Rodney wouldn't let it go. "Look, Adam, I don't care if you believe me. I guess I haven't given you any reason to trust me lately. But why should you trust Katie? You've never trusted a woman before. And I'm telling you as a friend, this is not the time to starting trusting one now. Especially this one."

Adam rose slowly to his feet, his anger tightly in check. "I'll stand up as your best man because I gave you my word. But as soon as the wedding is over, Katie and I are leaving."

"I've always admired your loyalty," Rodney said as Adam turned to leave the room. "I sincerely hope Katie O'Hara deserves it."

CHAPTER TWELVE

KATIE SAT AMONG THE ROWS of white folding chairs in the garden. She wore a lilac suit that Lorene Baker had insisted on loaning her for the wedding. Since she had nothing suitable to wear, Katie could hardly refuse. The skirt was a little loose in the waist, but a safety pin had solved that problem.

A harpist played lilting love songs on her strings as the groom and his best man took their places at the gazebo. Katie smiled at Adam, her stomach fluttering at the handsome picture he made in his tuxedo. Especially since she knew from recent experience how handsome he looked out of his tuxedo.

She still couldn't quite believe they'd made love last night. It was like a dream. A beautiful dream that she never wanted to end. Which was one reason she hadn't confided in him last night. She'd come so close. But her desire for him had overcome her conscience. And soon she'd been too swept away by passion to care.

This morning her conscience nagged at her, but so far she'd successfully ignored it. She'd barely had time to talk with Adam since she'd overslept, a natural consequence of making love all night, then had to hurry to prepare for the wedding. She'd seen him just long enough for a soul-wrenching kiss and a promise of more to come later.

He'd seemed a little distracted, but she blamed that on the harried last-minute wedding preparations. He wanted to leave as soon as the wedding was over, and she was ready to follow him anywhere.

But she wasn't ready to tell him the truth. Not yet. Not when their relationship was still so new and vulnerable. She couldn't risk losing him. Later, when she felt more secure about her identity—and about Adam's feelings for her—she would tell him everything.

Her silence on the subject bothered her more than she wanted to admit to herself. Was Katrina Lansing really this cowardly? This selfish? Something else nagged at her, too. A growing uneasiness that she was participating in Darla's deception by keeping her silence. Didn't Rodney deserve to know the truth?

The harpist played a flurry of notes to silence the buzz of the assembled wedding guests, then began plucking out the strains of Mendelssohn's "Wedding March." Katie rose with the rest of the guests as the bride made her way down the petal-strewn path. Darla's slender fingers clutched an elaborate wedding bouquet of gardenias and ivy but her expression was hidden beneath a filmy lace veil.

Katie bit her lip, suddenly wishing she'd said something to Rodney last night. But he'd been so defensive when she broached the subject of Darla. Would he have believed her?

She glanced at Adam, surprised to see his gaze on her instead of the bride. She looked away, torn with guilt and indecision. How easy it would be to quietly watch Rodney and Darla exchange vows. To keep her mouth shut.

That scared her almost as much as the alternative.

She slid into her seat as the wedding party turned their backs to the crowd and the minister began the ceremony. Her throat tightened in fear. Fear that she could be selfish enough *not* to do the right thing. Maybe Scarlett O'Hara could stand by in silence, looking out for her own interests. Maybe even the old Katrina Lansing. But what about the woman she was today?

And then came the words, before she had time to rationalize her actions or think of possible consequences.

"If there is anyone here," the minister intoned in his deep, solemn voice, "who knows of any reason why these two should not lawfully be married, let him speak now or forever hold his peace."

Almost against her volition, Katie rose slowly to her feet, her knees shaking. Sam waved to her. A low murmuring began in the crowd, swelling to gasps of astonishment. The minister looked up from his Bible. The wedding party turned, almost in unison.

Before Katie could open her mouth, Darla gave a loud, anguished cry. "No!" Then she ran sobbing from the garden into the house.

Rodney followed her at a run, calling her name. And Adam...

Adam stared at Katie as if he'd never seen her before. And never wanted to see her again.

THE MINISTER summoned Katie to Rodney's study, where the bride and groom, along with the rest of the wedding party, had already gathered.

Lorene Baker approached Katie as soon as she

walked through the door. "Two hundred thousand dollars," she hissed under her breath, "and all you have to do is play along and keep your mouth shut. You've already ruined my daughter's wedding day. Don't destroy the rest of her life."

Katie flinched at the venom in her tone. Darla did look devastated. She perched on the sofa, veil askew, her eyes swollen and red-rimmed. Rodney sat next to her, patting her hand and trying to soothe her.

Adam stood by the window, staring into the very meadow where they'd made love the night before. Her throat tightened. She had no choice but to tell him everything. To try to make him understand. But not here. Not now. She sat stiffly in a wing chair, the air around her crackling with tension.

"I'm certain," said the minister, after he'd gathered them all together, "that we can straighten out whatever misunderstandings have erupted here. Communication is the key."

He turned and looked expectantly at Katie. She cleared her throat, desperately wishing Adam would look at her. But he stayed at the window, his back rigid in his tuxedo jacket, as if he'd rather be anywhere other than in this room.

"I'm not sure where to begin," she said, nervously licking her dry lips. "I suppose I should have said something sooner."

A strangled sob rose from Darla, and she pressed her sodden handkerchief to her mouth.

"Look, I didn't think I had any choice," Katie said, feeling decidedly like a villain. "I couldn't keep this secret any longer."

"What secret?" the minister prodded.

"That I kissed her," Rodney interjected, then fell to his knees beside Darla. "I had a weak moment, Muffin. It didn't mean anything, truly. I know I should have told you, but you already seemed so stressed." He grabbed her lifeless hands in his. "Please say you'll forgive me."

Katie stifled a groan. Rodney would have to bring up that kiss now, when half the people in the room already wanted to tar and feather her.

"You cheated on my daughter?" Lorene said with a gasp.

"It was a kiss. One simple, meaningless kiss." Rodney rubbed Darla's hands between his palms. "At least it was to me. Obviously it meant more to Katie."

"Now wait just a minute," she cried, aware that Adam had turned from the window and was watching the scene before him with an air of detached curiosity.

"So now the truth comes out," Lorene declared, glaring at her. "You do want Rodney all to yourself. And the only way you can get him is to seduce him right out from under my daughter's nose!"

The minister cleared his throat. "Perhaps we all need a silent moment of contemplation."

Lorene wrenched her daughter's hand from Rodney's grasp. "I'd rather know exactly what went on between these two."

"Nothing!" Katie and Rodney exclaimed at the same time.

"I'm not interested in Rodney," Katie said, wanting to set the record straight. "I've never been *interested* in Rodney."

Adam raised a brow in disbelief. Too late she remembered her tireless interrogation of him when they'd arrived in Montana. She'd wanted to know every detail of Rodney Tate's life. "What I mean," she clarified, "is that I've never been romantically interested in him."

The minister leaned forward. "Then may I ask why you deemed it necessary to stop the wedding?"

Darla raised her head. "I'll answer that question." Her voice sounded weak and strained from crying. She hadn't spoken a word since the disruption of the wedding ceremony, but she turned to Rodney, dry-eyed and resolute. "I'd rather you hear this from me than anyone else."

Relief shone in Rodney's eyes now that his bride had come back to life. "Hear what, Muffin?"

Darla's hands clenched the voluminous skirt of her white wedding gown. "The truth. The awful truth about me."

Katie looked at the minister, then at Adam, who still had his gaze on her. "Maybe we should give them some privacy."

"No," Darla declared, holding up one hand to prevent them from leaving. "I want witnesses here so there's no doubt about the truth." Her chin quivered. "And so I don't chicken out at the last moment." She took a deep breath. "From now on I want only honesty between us."

"Darla," admonished her mother, "use your head."

Darla ignored Lorene, lifting her chin as she faced her fiancé. "Our entire relationship is based on a lie."

Rodney stiffened. "Are you saying...you don't love me?"

Darla gasped. "No! Of course I love you. I love you more than anything."

"But…" Rodney asked, in the doomed tone of a man who'd been through this before.

"You know that accident that brought us together?" she asked, sucking her lower lip between her teeth.

A shadow of a smile curved Rodney's mouth. "Your car backed into my car."

"Well, it was no accident."

His smile faded. "What do you mean?"

Her fists flexed on her taffeta skirt. "I mean I backed into you on purpose."

Katie closed her eyes. She'd had no idea. Poor Darla. Poor Rodney. She opened her eyes to see him sitting there in his tuxedo, slack-jawed and stunned.

"Don't blame Darla," Lorene Baker said gruffly. "I'm the one who encouraged her to go after you. We were having lunch in the hotel restaurant and you were seated at a nearby table. Darla was at loose ends, having just dropped out of college." Her nostrils flared. "She said she wanted a husband and babies. So I pointed you out, told her you were single, young and wealthy. And that it was just as easy to fall in love with a rich man as a poor man."

Rodney turned to Darla. "Is that true?"

"Yes." Her voice was barely a whisper.

The minister stepped forward. "Perhaps, in light of these circumstances, we should announce that the ceremony has been…indefinitely postponed. The guests have been kept waiting in the garden for quite some time now."

"No," Rodney said, his jaw clenched. "I want to

hear the rest of it. Was it your mother's idea to back into my car?''

Tears shimmered in Darla's eyes. ''No. That was my idea. I saw it in a movie once. A fender bender brought a man and a woman together and they fell in love. I know it sounds awful now, so callous and reckless. It *is* awful.''

Rodney stared at her for a long moment. ''But it worked.''

Darla nodded, one tear escaping and trailing down her cheek. ''It worked. I fell in love with you on our very first date.''

Rodney wiped her tear away, then broke into a grin. ''I can't tell you what a relief this is.''

She blinked at him. ''What do you mean? You're relieved you found out before you married me?''

''Hell, yes,'' Rodney exclaimed, looking more cheerful by the moment.

Katie briefly wondered if he was hysterical. She glanced at Adam, surprised to find his gaze still fixed on her. Heat crept up her cheeks until she finally had to turn away.

''Don't you see?'' Rodney said, shifting closer to Darla. ''I've been having attacks of cold feet for the last week because I thought you were so damn perfect. I'm not perfect, and I never will be. But now I've found out that neither are you.'' He laughed. ''I still can't believe you backed into my car on purpose. It cost me five hundred dollars in damages!''

Confusion wavered with relief on Darla's face. ''You're not mad?''

He grabbed her and kissed her soundly on the

lips. "I'm ecstatic! We make the perfect imperfect couple."

She grasped his shoulders, shaking him slightly. "Rodney, I don't think you understand. Our meeting was based on a lie."

"I understand perfectly. My money attracted you to me." His grin widened. "Guess what attracted me to you?"

"What?"

"Your money. Or rather, the Devlin money. I knew your mother handled the estate, and I thought she might be more likely to invest in ExecTec if I was dating her daughter."

Darla's face glowed. "Really?"

"Really. Guess what else attracted me to you?"

"What?"

"Your breasts. They're the main reason I asked you out on our first date. How's that for shallow?"

"They're fake," she admitted.

"I wear shoe lifts," Rodney confessed. "I'm really only five foot eight."

"That's just the right height for me." Tears spilled over Darla's cheeks as she wrapped her arms around Rodney's neck. "I love you, Tater."

He kissed her forehead. "I love you, too, Muffin. Now run upstairs and fix your makeup. We've got a wedding waiting for us."

Rodney and Darla walked from the room hand in hand. Katie watched them go without a word, her throat tight. There was no point in revealing Rodney as the missing Devlin heir. His grandfather's fortune might have brought them together, but it was evident they truly loved each other. Maybe it really was fate.

The minister turned to Katie and Adam, the only

two guests left in the room. "Well, it looks like I'll have to add another chapter to my book of unusual weddings." He picked up his Bible and turned to Katie. "Any more objections?"

She slowly shook her head. "No. I'm...glad it turned out this way."

"Me, too," the minister said with a chuckle, then headed out the door.

She could hear Adam's heavy footsteps behind her. "Are you really glad, Katie?"

She rose, turning to face him. "Yes," she replied, tilting her chin to meet his implacable gaze. "Although I can only guess what you must be thinking right now."

"Then let me enlighten you." He took a step closer to her until he stood so close she could smell the spicy scent of his aftershave. His nearness made her knees weak, made her remember how much she liked to touch him. And how easily he could melt her with just a touch, a kiss.

"I'm thinking you wanted Rodney from the very start," he said, his voice sounding even and calm. Almost too calm. "Maybe you heard some gossip about his trust fund. I know from personal experience how well gossip travels in Lightning Creek."

"Adam, I..." she began, but he didn't let her finish.

"I can only imagine your disappointment when Rodney failed to make an appearance at the auction. Did you know about my plans to attend his wedding before you bid on me?"

"Yes," she admitted.

"So I became your ticket to the Tate estate."

"Yes. But not for the reason you obviously think."

He folded his arms. "Then maybe you'd better explain it to me." He glanced at his watch. "And you'd better make it fast."

She took a deep breath. "I did want to meet Rodney. And that is the reason I bid on you at the auction. But I'm not a gold digger. And for your information, I was attracted to you from the moment we met."

"Which is why you threw yourself at Rodney."

She rolled her eyes. "I didn't throw myself at him. I let him kiss me. Once."

A muscled knotted in Adam's jaw. "This really isn't getting us anywhere."

"Then let me tell you *why* I let him kiss me." Katie stepped in front of him to prevent him from leaving. "I have amnesia, Adam. I recognized Rodney's picture in the bachelor brochure and I assumed he'd be able to fill in all the blanks in my memory. I was desperate to find him."

She could see the skepticism in his eyes, so she hurried on. "But when we arrived here, Rodney didn't seem to know me. I let him kiss me hoping it would refresh his memory."

"I thought you were the one who didn't remember anything?"

"I didn't. I still don't, except that my name is really Katrina Lansing, not Katie O'Hara. And I'm not a waitress, I'm an investigator. I was working on a case for Baker and Dunn when someone tried to kill me." The more words that spilled from her mouth, the more preposterous her story sounded, even to her. How could she possibly expect Adam to buy it?

"Is that all?"

"No." She licked her dry lips. "The other thing I know for certain is that...I love you."

A knock sounded on the door. The minister stuck his head in. "We're ready to start the ceremony. All we need is the best man."

"I'm coming," he said, and headed toward the door. He paused in the doorway, turning to Katie. "All I can say is...I hope you got your money's worth." Then he was gone.

Katie stared at the empty doorway. It wasn't quite a *Frankly, my dear, I don't give a damn*, but it was close enough.

"A TOAST to the bride and groom," Adam announced, holding his champagne flute in the air. He waited while the assembled guests at the reception grabbed their champagne glasses. Then he turned to the newly wedded couple at the head table. "Rodney and Darla, may your life together be as interesting and exciting as your wedding."

The crowd laughed while Rodney and Darla exchanged sheepish glances.

"I'm not much for poetry," Adam continued, "but I did come across something which I think fits this occasion." He cleared his throat. "'Life is like the weather, it's unpredictable and always changing. Love is a fragile flower, it needs sunshine and rain and tender care to grow.'" He raised his glass higher in the air. "Mr. and Mrs. Tate, I wish you plenty of sunshine ahead and lots of little sprouts."

The crowd applauded as Rodney and Darla, looking flushed and happy, stood up and kissed. Adam downed his champagne, then headed for the bar.

The wedding had passed by in a blur after Katie had blindsided him. He'd paid just enough attention to hand over the platinum wedding band at the appropriate moment. Now his duties were done and he wanted to succumb to amnesia himself, with the help of enough alcohol.

He tipped up his beer bottle, letting the cold lager wash down his throat. But it couldn't wash away the bitterness inside him. He'd wanted to believe her. Wanted to believe her so badly his gut ached with it. And that's what scared him.

Because he'd experienced that same gut-wrenching desperation before. Twenty years ago, to be exact. He still remembered his mother's words. Her cheerful reassurances. *It's only temporary. You'll like it here. Think of it as a vacation. We'll send for you.*

After the first six months her letters had stopped coming. After the first year, he'd stopped believing she'd ever come back for him. His mother had made her choice. She'd chosen her husband over her son.

Katie had made her choice, too. And Adam Harper wasn't going to be any woman's consolation prize. He drained his beer, then motioned to the bartender for another one.

"Hey," Rodney said, slapping him on the shoulder, "that was some toast. I didn't know you read poetry."

"It was required in Miss Lott's tenth-grade class, remember? You used to copy all my notes."

"So I did. Well, it was almost as good as that wedding vow you wrote."

"The one you didn't use," Adam reminded him.

Rodney's gaze sought out his bride. "I decided to create my own vow, use my own words to express my love. Especially since Darla seems to love me just the way I am."

Adam tipped up his beer. He didn't want to talk about love.

Rodney looked around the garden. "So where's Katie?"

He shrugged. "I don't know and I don't care. Sorry she caused so much trouble."

Rodney's brow rose. "You don't care?"

"After that little stunt she pulled at the wedding, how do you expect me to feel? Besides, you're the one who wanted to get rid of her as recently as yesterday."

"Only because I'd screwed up by kissing her and I was in a total panic that she'd tell Darla. I also felt guilty as hell. Look, if I'm honest with myself, I know she didn't come on to me. I mean, come on, she had *you*." Rodney sighed. "But I'm actually glad she stopped the ceremony. It gave Darla and me a chance to start our marriage with honesty between us. And frankly, I have high hopes that we really will live happily ever after."

"You make Katie sound like some kind of saint."

Rodney stared at him. "You know, I used to think you were smart about women, but now I believe you're even dumber than me."

"And I'd have to agree with you."

Sam Duncan, looking more than a little uncomfortable in a gray flannel suit, walked up and clapped Rodney on the shoulder. "Congratulations, Tate. You're a lucky man."

Rodney smiled. "You're right, as always, Sam."

Sam chuckled, then turned to Adam. "I need to head back to Wyoming soon, but I'd like to say goodbye to Katie before I go. Do you know where I can find her?"

"No." Adam clenched his jaw. How could he possibly forget about Katie when everybody kept reminding him of her?

Sam grinned. "Why do I have the feeling someone stole your piece of pie?"

"I've given up sweets," Adam said wryly, realizing Marge must have told him about their pie conversation.

Rodney darted a confused look between the two of them, then turned to Sam. "We don't have any pie, just wedding cake."

"That just happens to be my favorite kind of cake," Sam said. "In fact, I think I'll go grab a couple of pieces for the road."

Rodney watched him walk away, then he turned to Adam. "What's with the pie?"

Darla's arrival saved him from replying. She hooked her hand around her new husband's arm. "Did you miss me?"

Rodney answered her question with a searing kiss, and Adam couldn't deny the tiny twinge of envy at their obvious happiness. He looked away and took another swig of beer.

"Tater, please," Darla gasped, breaking away from his embrace with a giggle. "I've got to give Adam a message."

Adam lowered his beer. "From who?"

"Corinne Sullivan. She'd like you to call her as soon as possible."

Grateful for an opportunity to be alone, Adam took his beer with him into the privacy of Rodney's study. He leaned back in the leather chair, then dialed Corinne's number on the cordless phone. The line was picked up on the first ring. "Hey, Corinne, this is Harper."

"Adam, I've been trying to reach you for the last hour."

"They disconnected all the phones during the wedding ceremony," he explained. "What's up?"

"I finally got some more information on Katie O'Hara."

He sat up in the chair. "Tell me."

"Well, that psychic came out to the office yesterday and did a reading."

He rolled his eyes. "I thought you had something *relevant* to report. Don't tell me you believe all that mumbo jumbo. And please don't tell me you paid for her services."

"Twenty bucks, but it was worth it. I used to be a skeptic, too, but I saw too many cases solved down at the department to call it coincidence. It's not like we had any other leads."

"All right. What did you find out?"

"Well, she started by reading the aura around the file cabinet with the missing personnel files. It was pink."

"Pink for girls, blue for boys?" he quipped.

"Your cynicism is showing again. Now quit interrupting. Anyway, a pink aura basically means that the thief is benign. In other words, she's not a danger to others. Although the psychic did sense a possible threat to the thief herself."

He snorted. "First of all, there must be ten people

that walk by that filing cabinet every day. How can this psychic pick out the aura of a woman who hasn't been there for two months? And second, what possible danger could there be to the thief? Slamming her hand in the file drawer?''

"That's what I asked Betty."

"The psychic's name is Betty?"

"I know. You'd think she'd pick something a little more exotic, like Natasha or Delfina. Anyway, she didn't have any answers for me, just a sense of a pink aura threatened by a black cloud."

"So the reading was a bust."

"I thought so, too, until we started talking about purses."

"Now you've really lost me. What do purses have to do with this investigation?"

"Absolutely nothing. We were walking to the parking lot together and I told her how much I liked her purse. It was more like a basket, actually, but woven together with wheat straw. She told me her second cousin Irene makes them."

"So?"

"So we start talking, and I find out Irene lives in Lightning Creek, Wyoming."

"Small world."

"Getting smaller all the time. She's married to Sheriff Reese Hatcher."

Adam's fingers curled more tightly around the telephone receiver. "The one who wouldn't talk about the accident."

"It seems he talks to his wife. Of course, she doesn't gossip to anyone local, but what harm is there in telling her cousin in Chicago about a few cases? Especially since her cousin is a psychic who might be able to help crack the tough ones.''

He grinned. ''If you were here right now, I'd kiss you.''

''No offense, boss, but I'd rather have a raise.''

''Done.'' He drew a notepad toward him, then pulled a pen out of the center drawer. ''Now tell me everything you know.''

''The woman who bought you at the bachelor auction is not Katie O'Hara.''

''So who is she?''

''I don't know. *Nobody* knows, including the woman herself. She woke up after the accident with amnesia.''

He closed his eyes. ''Oh, no.''

''Oh, yes. Apparently, the doctors were stumped. She'd sustained a severe concussion, but there was no other physical reason for her condition.''

''She seems perfectly fine to me,'' he said, remembering the way she'd bantered with him. Danced a rumba. Made love with him under the stars. ''She obviously remembers how to do all the basics, like cook and tie her shoes.''

''That's what's so strange about this case. According to Irene, one of the doctors hypothesized that her amnesia was a result of an emotional trauma. He thought it might be a coping mechanism to block out something she didn't want to remember.''

''But why keep it a secret?'' he asked, not quite ready to accept the truth. Or the fact that he'd been a complete jerk. ''You'd think she'd want people to know she had amnesia. Someone might have come forward who could identify her.''

"Someone like the jerk who shot her tires?"

Adams gut clenched. "Did you say *shot?*"

"That's right, boss. And Sheriff Hatcher doesn't think it was an accident. Maybe the lady kept her secret because she didn't know who she could trust."

Could he blame her? When she'd finally confided in him, he'd thrown that trust right back in her face.

Adam rang off, then rubbed his hand across his jaw, wondering how he'd let his past taint his future. His mother had lied and deceived him because she didn't want him to make a fuss about staying at Lost Springs. She'd always believed decent people didn't show their emotions. Even when his father died, she hadn't cried at the funeral and had been exasperated with Adam when he'd broken down at the cemetery.

Maybe that's why she'd taken the dog with her instead. Alfred had been very low maintenance in the emotion department. A full bowl of dog food and water kept him content. He didn't try her patience or ask to be tucked in at night.

For the first time he wondered what had made his mother that way. When his father was alive, she used to laugh more. Hug Adam more. Even cry at sappy television movies, though she'd always tried to hide her tears. But after the motorcycle accident that had killed his father, she'd closed off that part of herself. She'd seldom shown any emotion, except fear when she couldn't pay the gas bill or when the telephone company laid her off.

The fear had disappeared when she'd married Adam's stepfather. But the laughter and the hugs and the tears never came back. Probably because she'd married a man even more unemotional than herself. A man who hadn't wanted to deal with a rebellious, troubled stepson.

Adam buried his head in his hands. He was turning out just like them. Someone afraid to experience the full range of his emotions because he might end up getting hurt. He'd turned his back on Katie because she'd made him feel betrayed and confused. He hadn't given her the benefit of the doubt. Hell, he hadn't even considered she might have her reasons for not trusting him.

He'd blown it. He hoped it wasn't too late to repair the damage. He still had questions, but this time he'd ask for answers instead of demanding them. This time he'd listen with his heart instead of jumping to the worst possible conclusions.

Rodney stuck his head through the open door of the study. "Hey, best man, I need you to cause a distraction." He grinned. "We're ready to leave for the honeymoon."

Adam placed his palms on the desk and slowly rose to his feet. "I need to talk to Katie."

"I'm sure she's around here someplace. Unless she decided to walk to Butte."

He wouldn't put it past her. Or more likely, she'd stow away in the car of a departing wedding guest. After the way Adam had treated her, she probably never wanted to see him again. He looked at Rodney. "How long did it take you to fall in love with Darla?"

He grinned. "About five minutes. Why? Is wedding fever catching?"

Adam scowled. "I've only known Katie five days."

"Yeah, but I think you've been looking for a woman like her all your life."

Rodney was right. But did that mean he was ready for a commitment? Marriage? He mentally shook himself. He couldn't even remember what Katie's real name was. When he proposed, he wanted it to be to the right woman.

Now he just had to find her.

CHAPTER THIRTEEN

KATIE COULDN'T LEAVE without saying goodbye to Wiley.

She'd made arrangements with Rodney's foreman to feed and care for Wiley until the young coyote was grown enough to be set free. Adam was right. Wiley belonged in the wild. Katie couldn't use her own loneliness and heartache as an excuse to keep him caged up any longer than necessary.

She'd changed out of Lorene's suit and into her old reliable denim dress. The caterer had agreed to give her a ride to Butte as soon as the wedding luncheon was over. Until then, she planned to stay out of sight. She absolutely did not want to see Adam again. Especially the hurt and disillusionment he couldn't hide in his blue eyes.

The stable provided a welcome relief from the hot sun, and Katie inhaled the fragrant scent of fresh-cut hay when she walked through the door. A scent that made her think of wet kisses and slow hands and loving Adam.

She shook the image away just in time to see Wiley, his sharp nose through the slats of the gate, lifting the latch on his pen.

"Caught you in the act," she said, hurrying toward his pen to secure it once more. Then she set the shopping bag containing her few meager belongings on the straw-covered floor.

Wiley backed away from the gate, yipping excitedly at the sight of her.

"Yes, I brought you a treat." She reached into the shopping bag and pulled out a meaty T-bone sealed in plastic wrap, courtesy of the caterer. Katie tore the plastic away and tossed the bone in Wiley's food dish. He immediately began gnawing on it, his motley tail wagging cheerfully back and forth.

Tears stung her eyes even as she smiled. "Somehow I don't think you're going to miss me as much as your treats."

It was probably stupid to cry over leaving a coyote. Especially since she'd only discovered him a few days ago. But who else did she have in her life? Certainly not Adam. He'd made it clear how much he abhorred any kind of deception. And she'd lied to him since the moment they met. Was it any wonder he didn't believe her amnesia story?

"I should have told him sooner," she murmured. "I should have trusted him." But she hadn't known then the depth of his honor and integrity. And she'd been so scared. So alone. She hadn't known how easy it would be to fall in love with him. Or how hard it would be to lose him.

And she had no one to blame but herself.

She swiped at her eyes, then reached into the pocket of her denim dress for a tissue. For all her precautions, she'd still ended up with nothing. She didn't have her full memory back, and she'd never have Adam.

He'd thrown her love right back in her face, along

with the truth, believing neither one. And why should he? Especially when he'd suspected her motives from the start.

"Tomorrow is another day," Katie whispered. It didn't make her feel any better. She wasn't Katie Scarlett O'Hara, a fictional character created from an author's vivid imagination. She was Katrina Lansing, a woman with a shoddy memory and a broken heart.

She wadded the tissue in her hand as she gazed at her coyote, who was completely oblivious of anything except his bone. He'd chewed it clean and commenced licking it thoroughly. "I'm a mess, Wiley. You're probably better off without me."

"Am I interrupting something?" Lorene Baker's cultured, slightly nasal tone seem incongruous with the rustic interior and earthy aromas of the stable.

Katie took one last swipe at her eyes before turning. "Not at all. I was just telling my—"

"Oh, yes. Rodney mentioned you had a coyote out here." She wrinkled her nose as she peered into Wiley's pen. "Ugly little thing."

A primal instinct to defend her young, regardless of the species, rose inside Katie. "He's still recovering from a serious injury. If his fur looks a little scraggly, it's because the veterinarian had to trim it to treat his wounds. He's really very intelligent for his age." She leaned over to scratch behind his ear. "Would you like to pet him?"

Wiley reacted with a primitive instinct of his own, growling low in his throat to indicate sole ownership of his delectable bone.

Lorene stepped away from the pen. "Perhaps another time. I'd like to take care of business first."

Katie turned to face her. "What business?"

Lorene opened her ecru leather handbag. "Shall we call it your…compensation for keeping quiet about Rodney's inheritance?"

"It hardly seemed necessary to go into detail when Rodney admitted pursuing Darla for *her* money. Or should I say *his* money. When do you plan to tell him he's the Devlin heir?"

Lorene shrugged. "Six months, perhaps a year. Long enough to make certain the marriage can't be ended without earning my daughter a huge settlement. Hopefully, there will be a child by that time." Her eyes shone with unconcealed avarice. "A permanent tie to the Devlin fortune."

The callousness of the remark made Katie blanch. "Don't you care about your daughter's happiness?"

"Money can buy plenty of happiness. And strangely enough, Darla has fallen in love with the man. Chances are that it won't last. It certainly didn't with her father and me." Lorene held out the check. "Here is a little chunk of happiness of your very own."

Katie stared at the check, mesmerized by the number of zeros. There was enough money there for her to start over anywhere in the country. Enough to hire a fleet of private detectives to find her past. Or psychiatrists. She'd never have to wait tables or flirt for tips again. But for some reason, she couldn't bring herself to take it.

Sensing her hesitation, Lorene pushed the check into her hand. "Take it, Katrina. You've earned it.

Without you, we might never have found Alfred Devlin's long-lost son.'' She smiled. ''My new son-in-law.''

''Alfred who?'' Katie rubbed her temple with her fingertips. Lorene's expensive floral perfume was starting to give her a headache. Even the balmy breeze drifting through the open stable windows didn't dissipate it.

''Ah. Very good.'' Lorene rewarded her with a nod. ''The sooner you forget all about Alfred Monroe Devlin, the better. Too bad his father couldn't do the same. He wasted too much of his life searching for his ungrateful son.''

The impact of Lorene's words made her stagger against the gate. *Alfred Monroe Devlin?* She reached out to steady herself, shaken by a sudden, blinding pain in her head.

Lorene scowled. ''What's the matter with you?''

She waited a moment for the pain to recede. ''Alfred Monroe Devlin. Are you certain that's his name?''

''Of course. You should know it as well as anyone.''

Katie only knew that the world had tilted on its axis. She stared at Lorene, shock straining her voice. ''Rodney Tate isn't the Devlin heir.''

Lorene's scowl deepened. ''Don't be ridiculous.''

''It's true,'' Katie said, still not quite able to believe it herself. Or how easily the missing pieces from her past began to snap into place. ''Rodney seemed like the logical choice because his parents' bodies were never recovered after that drowning accident. So no identification was possible.''

"And neither parent had any surviving relatives other than their son," Lorene said dryly. "I've already read your report. You don't need to repeat it."

Katie looked at her. "It was only a preliminary report. I never found any definitive proof that Rodney Tate was the Devlin heir. I'd discovered that Alfred Devlin had ended up in Wyoming, then taken an alias. I never discovered what that alias was. Until now."

Lorene arched a perfect blond brow. "Tate, I presume?"

"No. Harper. Alfred Harper." Katie swallowed hard. "The Devlin heir is Adam Harper."

Lorene snorted. "How convenient for you. I suppose you concocted this scheme shortly before you bought him at that bachelor auction?"

Katie slowly shook her head. "I didn't realize the truth until just now. Adam told me...about his father. His name was Alfred Harper."

"Coincidence," Lorene snapped.

"Adam's middle name is Monroe."

Lorene paled. "That doesn't prove anything."

"No. But a DNA test will. And I'd be willing to wager every penny of the Devlin fortune that Adam Harper is the true heir."

Lorene unsnapped her handbag once again. "Exactly how many zeros will it take to forget this preposterous theory of yours?"

"I'll never forget it." Katie tore the check in half and let it flutter to the floor. "Just like I'll never accept one dime of your money, Mrs. Baker. Adam deserves to know the truth."

Lorene sighed. "I knew it was a mistake to hire

an investigator with scruples.'' Then she pulled a small pistol out of her handbag. ''Fortunately, it's a mistake I can rectify.''

ADAM COULDN'T FIND HER anywhere. This was the second time in less than a week that she'd disappeared without a trace. It was getting to be a bad habit. Not to mention driving him crazy. Her room was empty, her clothes and makeup gone. Yet no one had seen her leave.

He'd driven the Blazer ten miles down the highway in case she truly had decided to walk. Adam hoped she wasn't foolish enough to hitchhike. Not that she'd have much luck on this remote stretch of road, which averaged about one car an hour.

When he didn't see any sign of her, he circled back to the house. The reception was winding down, the tables littered with empty plates and champagne flutes. The guests were gathered in small groups, laughing and talking together. Rodney and Darla were slow-dancing on the brick patio, sans music, and staring dreamily into each others' eyes.

Katie was nowhere in sight.

Rodney finally tore his besotted gaze from his bride and motioned to Adam. ''We're ready to leave. Do you mind causing that distraction so we're not subjected to the traditional barrage of rice?''

''Rice gives Tater a rash,'' Darla explained, gathering the skirt of her wedding gown for a quick exit.

Adam was glad to oblige. He walked to the center of the terrace, tapping a spoon against a champagne flute. ''Ladies and gentlemen, may I have your attention. I'm looking for a woman.''

The crowd laughed as several of the women in the audience raised their hands.

"A particular woman," Adam clarified. "Her name is...." He hesitated, uncertain what exactly to call her. "She goes by Katie O'Hara." He held his hand at shoulder level. "She's about this tall and has red hair and brown eyes."

"I'll take one of those, too," shouted one of the ushers, to the amusement of the crowd.

Out of the corner of his eye, he saw Rodney and Darla duck through the hedge. They'd soon be on their way to a month-long cruise in the South Seas. Adam suddenly wished he could get Katie on a cruise ship. At least that would limit how far she could wander away from him.

"If anyone knows where I can find her," Adam continued, "please let me know."

He'd just set down the spoon and champagne flute when a redhead wearing a short black skirt and a white lace blouse walked up to him. "Perhaps I can be of service."

"Thanks for the offer, but I'm afraid you misunderstood. I'm looking for a specific redhead."

She smiled. "I believe you're the one who misunderstood. I'm the caterer, and I just saw Katie in the kitchen twenty minutes ago. She's catching a ride with me into Butte as soon as the reception ends."

His pulse quickened. "So she's in the kitchen." That was the one place he *hadn't* checked.

The caterer shook her head. "Not anymore. She dug some meat scraps out of the trash, then headed out the door. She said she was going to visit a friend until I was ready to go.''

Meat scraps. That could only mean one thing. *Wiley*. The stables had been the first place Adam had looked for her. Had they missed each other somewhere along the way? There was only one way to find out.

''If she comes back here, don't let her get away,'' Adam called to the caterer as he turned and jogged toward the stables. He was slightly out of breath when he reached the stable door.

He couldn't breathe at all when he saw the gun aimed at Katie's heart.

KATIE STARED straight at the gun barrel, wondering what she'd done to deserve this. Life had been much easier when she didn't remember anything. Not as exciting, but definitely easier. Although *exciting* wasn't quite the word she'd use to describe this particular situation. *Terrifying* was more accurate.

She stood frozen in place, aware of Wiley scratching on his gate behind her and making small whimpers in his throat. He wanted out of his pen. She wanted out, too. Her gaze flew to the open stable door, and she blinked twice when she saw Adam Harper standing frozen in the doorway.

If she made a run for it, he could be caught in the line of fire. She swallowed hard, and her gaze darted to the gun in Lorene's steady, manicured hand.

''You won't shoot me,'' Katie whispered.

Lorene smiled, a cool grimace that made Katie's stomach twist into a knot. ''Please don't underestimate me. I'm a woman who always gets exactly what she wants.''

''I don't think you want to go to prison for murder.''

''That's assuming quite a lot. The first is that I will be arrested. The second is that a jury will convict me. Fortunately, my business brings me into contact with several masterful defense attorneys.'' Lorene hooked her handbag over her wrist. ''But naturally, I would prefer to avoid any negative publicity.''

''Naturally,'' Katie echoed, her voice dry as sawdust. She saw movement out of the corner of her eye. Adam was creeping inside the stable, one painstaking inch at a time. Closer to Katie. Closer to the danger.

She shifted a half step to the right, trying to block Lorene's view of the doorway. ''I can certainly see how shooting me might be bad for business.''

Lorene sighed. ''It would be much easier on both of us if I could just find a way to convince you to keep your mouth shut.''

Realization washed over Katie. ''You tried that once before. The Devlin relatives weren't to blame for that car accident. It was you.''

''I never meant for you to be physically harmed,'' Lorene replied, confirming Katie's suspicions. ''Although I'll admit I was quite irritated when you refused to back off the investigation. I was perfectly happy with the results of the preliminary report.''

''That's when Darla met Rodney.''

Lorene nodded. ''Thanks to some clever foresight and planning on her mother's part. Darla may not be the perfect daughter, but she has always been quite susceptible to the power of suggestion. Then you conveniently disappeared.''

"I was almost killed," Katie whispered.

"Regrettable," Lorene concurred. "That cretin I hired misunderstood my instructions. I wanted him to put an end to your search, not to you personally." She shifted her weight to her other foot, keeping the gun trained on Katie. "I assumed when you stayed on in Lightning Creek that investigative work had lost its appeal. Imagine my surprise when you showed up for the wedding."

But Katie barely heard her. Memories came crashing over her as if a dam had broken. She closed her eyes, overwhelmed by the intensity of the pain in her head. After a dizzying moment, it cleared. Then her past fell firmly, and completely, into place.

Tears stung her eyes. She was Katrina Rose Lansing, born and raised in Grand Junction, Colorado. Her parents still lived there. So did a string of four lovable little sisters. The tears spilled over as joy mingled with relief. She'd kissed her first boy at a homecoming dance. Earned her bachelor's degree in criminal justice from Colorado State University. Then she'd decided to see the rest of the country, living first in Atlanta, Georgia, then Austin, Texas, before finally hiring on at the law firm of Baker and Dunn in Denver.

The Devlin case had been her first for them. And her last. All too clearly, she remembered her growing fear in the days before the accident. The eerie sense that someone was following her. Her dogged determination to see the case through to the end, even though Lorene Baker had ordered her to stop the investigation.

Had her amnesia been an unconscious act of self-preservation? A way to erase her involvement in the case before Lorene and her hired thug finished the job? Katie didn't know the answers to those questions, and at this point, she didn't care. She finally had her life back again. Now she just hoped she could keep it.

Lorene stared at her, misinterpreting the cause of the tears wetting her cheeks. "I see you're finally beginning to understand the gravity of this situation." A light suddenly gleamed in her pale green eyes. "Perhaps there is a way to acquire your silence. After all, pet-napping isn't a felony." She turned toward Wiley's pen. "Just how much do you love your mangy coyote?"

Katie cried out as Lorene aimed the gun at Wiley. He jumped on his hind legs, his front paws pressing against the gate. It swung open, crashing into Lorene's gun hand. Her arm flailed as a shot exploded into the air.

Katie hit the plank floor, using her feet to sweep Lorene's legs out from under her. The older woman fell on her backside with a pained grunt, the gun bobbling in her hand.

The next moment Adam had Lorene pinned to the floor, her arms behind her back and her gun stuck in his cummerbund. He twisted a length of twine around her wrists, binding them tightly together. A crowd had gathered outside the stable, obviously drawn by the sound of gunfire.

"Call the police," Adam shouted. Then he moved

to Katie's side, his worried gaze scanning the length of her body. "Are you all right?"

She nodded, her movements jerky. "I'm...fine," she replied, her teeth chattering. When she tried to stand, her knees gave out and she fell into a faint in Adam's arms.

Right where she belonged.

"DAMN IT," Adam roared, pacing the faded brown tile floor in the Butte police station. "How much longer is this going to take?" Katie had barely revived from her faint when the police had arrived, taking Lorene and Katie to the station in separate police cruisers for questioning. Adam had followed at breakneck speed in the Blazer, only to be kept cooling his heels for the last hour.

The desk sergeant, a portly blond woman with blue eyes and matching blue mascara, looked at him. "Miss Lansing has requested counsel. We're waiting for her attorney to arrive."

"Attorney?" Adam stopped pacing and placed both palms on the desk. "Lorene Baker is the one who needs an attorney, not Katie. She was the victim!"

"Mrs. Baker has also requested counsel," the sergeant added helpfully. Then she tilted forward in her chair, her voice lowered to a confidential whisper. "However, this is the first time an alleged perp and her victim ever requested the *same* attorney. Talk about a conflict of interest."

Before Adam could ask which attorney they'd requested, his answer walked through the door: Harvard Dunn, sixtyish and balding, still dressed in the expensive, tailored gray suit he'd worn to Rodney and Darla's wedding.

Dunn greeted Adam with a curt nod, then turned to the desk sergeant. "I'm here to see my client."

"Which one?" Adam inquired wryly.

The sergeant shot him an exasperated look, then tapped a few keys on her computer keyboard. "Mrs. Baker is still being processed. However, Miss Lansing is available in witness room three."

"I'm going with you," Adam stated.

Dunn shook his head. "I conduct all my consultations in private."

"Tough. I haven't seen Katie since they loaded her into that police cruiser. She looked pale. Scared." He raked his fingers through his hair. "Now I need to know she's all right. And I need to tell her..." His voice trailed off. He didn't want a go-between to tell her what was in his heart.

Dunn patted his shoulder. "I'll tell her you want to see her as soon as possible. Just give me a few moments."

Adam could barely resist the urge to follow Dunn into the witness room. He began pacing the floor again, wondering how much longer he could stand waiting to see her.

The desk sergeant held the telephone receiver to her ear. "Excuse me, Mr. Harper. We're still unable to locate Mr. and Mrs. Tate. Do you have another telephone number where we might reach them?"

He'd already given the police Rodney's cellular number. If the newlyweds didn't want to be disturbed, then he wasn't going to be the one responsible for interrupting their honeymoon. Darla would find out soon enough about her mother's duplicity. Somehow he doubted she'd be surprised.

"No, I don't. They're on their honeymoon. Since they left before the incident occurred, I doubt they can contribute anything more to the investigation."

The sergeant pursed her lips. "The crime did take place at Mr. Tate's residence. He should be informed."

Adam gave her the name of Rodney's attorney, and she seemed satisfied with that information. He glanced at his watch, telling himself he'd only wait five more minutes. Then he was going in after her.

"Mr. Harper?"

Adam turned to see Harvard Dunn standing outside witness room three.

"Katie is ready to see you now."

CHAPTER FOURTEEN

KATIE DIDN'T KNOW she was holding her breath until Adam walked into the room. He looked gorgeously rumpled, with his dark hair standing on end and his black bow tie askew. He glanced at the plainclothes policeman sitting at the end of the long conference table, then his gaze centered on Katie. She gulped at the indefinable emotion smoldering in his blue eyes.

"Have a seat, Mr. Harper," the cop said, flipping a page in his notebook. His brown suit was slightly wrinkled, and he had a pair of bifocals perched on his nose. "I'm Detective Cohen, and I've asked Mr. Dunn to sit in on this session, too. Miss O'Hara will be giving us her official statement, and I'd like you to add anything you deem appropriate."

Adam pulled out a chair and sat across the table from Katie. Then he turned to the cop. "I already gave a statement to a police officer out at the Tate estate."

The detective pushed a lock of his unruly gray hair off his forehead. "Yes, I've read it. We're hoping you may be able to provide some additional details once you've heard the full story."

"The full story?" He shifted his gaze to Katie. "I don't understand. Why would Lorene Baker hold you at gunpoint? Your blueberry muffins weren't that bad."

She smiled, knowing soon he wouldn't be cracking jokes. She'd be lucky if he didn't want to strangle her.

"Please, Mr. Harper," Detective Cohen chided, "we have some serious allegations here." Then he nodded to Katie. "Anytime you're ready, Miss O'Hara."

"It's Lansing," Katie reminded him. She didn't blame him for being confused. She was still a little confused herself. Except about her feelings for Adam. She loved him. And she stood a very good chance of losing him.

"That's right," Detective Cohen muttered, scratching out O'Hara at the top of the witness form, then printing Lansing above it. "I keep forgetting."

"That was my problem, too," she said, beginning her story. "I was involved in a car accident two months ago, which resulted in amnesia." She couldn't look at Adam. She didn't want to see the same disbelief in his eyes that she'd seen this morning. "I could remember how to do all the everyday things, like make a bed and drive a car, but I remembered nothing of the people or events from my past."

"I don't know much about amnesia," Detective Cohen admitted. "Is that unusual?"

Katie nodded. "The doctors were stumped. They suggested my amnesia might not be caused by a physical reason, but a psychological one."

"Like a repressed memory?" Cohen asked.

"Except I repressed everything," Katie replied.

She took a deep breath, forcing herself to face Adam. "What I didn't remember is that a week before the accident I gained access to Adam Harper's personnel file at ExecTec."

Adam's jaw sagged. "You're the leggy redhead?"

She gave him a shaky smile. "Guess I fit the description, after all."

He didn't smile back. Instead he looked… stunned. Katie hurried on with her story before she completely lost her nerve. "I also tried to con my way into his penthouse apartment, but the doorman didn't fall for it. I wanted access to his personal belongings—letters, pictures, anything I could get my hands on. Now I cringe at some of my methods, but before the accident I was a very determined lady."

Adam stared at her. "Why?"

Harvard Dunn cleared his throat. "I think we're getting a little ahead of ourselves. It's a rather complicated story." He turned to Katie. "Perhaps you should begin when Baker and Dunn hired you."

She nodded stiffly, all her hopes fading at the stark expression on Adam's face. "Three months ago, I was hired by Lorene Baker as a special investigator for the law firm of Baker and Dunn. My first case assignment was to find the lost heir to the Devlin fortune."

Detective Cohen looked up from his notepad to Adam. "You've heard of Ox Devlin?"

"Who hasn't?" Adam replied, breaking his long silence. "He was a shady industrialist who amassed a small fortune during the last six decades."

"Small isn't quite accurate in this case," Mr. Dunn said dryly. "He was worth millions. Unfortunately, he died intestate because he insisted his fortune should go to his grandson. A grandson some of the distant Devlin relatives called a figment of the old man's imagination."

Katie picked up where Dunn left off. "Only the grandson is real. I traced him to the Lost Springs Ranch for Boys near Lightning Creek, Wyoming. Then I sent a preliminary report to Lorene Baker that Rodney Tate was the most likely candidate." She saw by his expression the moment Adam made the connection.

A light flashed in his blue eyes. "Lorene knew Rodney was going to be a multimillionaire. That's why she encouraged Darla to go after him."

Katie nodded. "As far as Lorene was concerned, the investigation was over, even though I didn't have any solid proof at that point."

Dunn leaned his forearms on the table. "The difficulty, you see, is that Ox Devlin's son had renounced his father and his inheritance almost forty years ago. He apparently changed his name and completely cut all ties to his family."

"Except his sister," Katie interjected, seeing the confusion in Adam's eyes. "Cynthia Devlin kept her brother's new identity a well-guarded secret—until his death in 1979. Then she informed her father that the entire family had been killed in a tragic accident. She knew it would be her dead brother's wish to keep his son from the corrupting influence of his grandfather."

Adam snorted. "Did she really think her nephew

would be better off at a home for boys than with family?''

Katie drew in a deep breath. ''Apparently so. When she learned her nephew had been placed at Lost Springs, she made a generous donation to the ranch every year from 1979 to 1984, the year of her death. But even though Ox believed his grandson was still alive, all his investigations turned up cold.''

Detective Cohen furiously scribbled notes on the witness form. ''Until yours?''

Katie nodded, her palms growing damp as she got closer to the truth. Adam looked somewhat interested, but impatient. He had no idea of the other bombshell she was about to drop in his life. ''I'm the one who traced Cynthia Devlin's donations to Lost Springs and tied them together with the year she reported her brother's death. A process of elimination turned up Rodney Tate as the likely heir. Both his parents had died that year in a drowning accident, and their bodies were never recovered.''

''So there was no way to make a positive identification,'' Adam concluded.

Katie nodded. ''Lorene ordered me off the case, satisfied with my findings. But I wasn't satisfied, so I kept digging.'' Her fingers clenched the arms of her chair. ''Until that car accident on Shoshone Highway.''

The cop looked up from his notes. ''Is that when you sustained the alleged memory loss?''

Katie flinched at the word *alleged.* ''Yes. My memory didn't fully return until today. That's when Lorene considered me a serious threat.''

"Even after Rodney and Darla were legally married?" Cohen asked.

Katie nodded. "Yes."

Adam sat forward in his chair, his brow crinkled in bewilderment. "But why?"

She took a deep breath. "Because the Devlin heir isn't Rodney, after all."

Adam scowled. "Then who is it?"

"You."

"ME?" ADAM STARED at Katie, wondering if she was still feeling dizzy. That was it. She must be confused. "That's impossible."

"It's true," she insisted. "I didn't consider you as a possibility at first because your guardianship papers at Lost Springs had your father's signature on them."

"My father couldn't have signed them," Adam said, slightly unnerved by the tone of certainty in her voice. He didn't remember seeing any guardianship papers. Of course, he'd been too distraught to notice much of anything—except his mother and stepfather driving away.

"I know. Your stepfather signed them. And even though it looked as if Rodney was the logical choice as the Devlin heir, I still had some unanswered questions. That's why I conducted that search of your files in Chicago. I was hoping to find some clues to the identity of your real father."

"And did you?"

"Not then." She licked her pale lips. "I put it all together today, when my memory finally returned."

He didn't want to hear it. Instead he wanted to

gather Katie in his arms and escape from all the questions and explanations. Forget about everything except the two of them. But Adam Harper wasn't a coward. He could face the truth. Even if it meant his own father had deceived him about his past and his family background. "Tell me."

"The name of Ox Devlin's son was Alfred Monroe Devlin. I know your middle name is Monroe. And your father's name was—"

"Alfred," he finished for her, a dull roaring in his ears. "Alfred Harper." Except that wasn't his father's name. Not his real name—something he'd never revealed to his son.

"I'm sorry, Adam," Katie said softly.

"I think congratulations, not condolences, are in order," Dunn said. "DNA tests will be required, but once we verify all of this, Mr. Harper will be a very rich man." He leaned toward Adam, lowering his voice a notch. "You'll need to hire an attorney so we can be certain the transfer of the Devlin estate is done properly. As a trustee of the estate, I'll be happy to help in any way I can."

The detective stood up. "Before we get into all that, we have a few other matters to settle. Do you wish to press charges, Mr. Harper?"

Adam shook his head to clear it. "Charges?"

"Against Miss O'Hara...I mean Miss Lansing. There is some evidence of criminal activity, although I'd venture a guess it would only be a misdemeanor." He shrugged. "Of course, it's out of my jurisdiction. Perhaps you'd rather wait until you get back to Chicago to settle the matter."

"Fine," Adam replied, barely comprehending his

words. He was still trying to digest the truth about
his family. His mother obviously hadn't known
about their wealthy connections. Adam had no doubt
she would have turned to them for financial help,
despite the rift.

If she had, his life might have turned out completely different. He would have had all the privi-
leges and perks of the Devlin name. No hardships.
No struggles. No Lost Springs Ranch. The place that
had honed him into the successful, independent man
he was today.

Somehow he couldn't find any room in his heart
for regret. His sojourn at Lost Springs had given him
a lot. Most recently, it had given him Katie. And
he'd put off telling her how much she meant to him
long enough.

But he was too late. When Adam finally emerged
from his shell-shocked state, he looked up to find
only Detective Cohen and Harvard Dunn in the
room.

Katie was gone.

TWO WEEKS LATER, Adam sat in his office at
ExecTec in Chicago, surrounded by lawyers. His
hand ached from signing so many papers and legal
documents. Documents that proclaimed him the legal heir to the Devlin fortune. The preliminary blood
and DNA tests provided conclusive evidence that he
was the son of the late Alfred Monroe Devlin.

Adam wondered if his father ever regretted cut-
ting off all ties with his family. Perhaps time would
have eventually healed old wounds. Despite the
family breach and his grandfather's reputation,

Adam planned to manage the Devlin fortune in a way that would have made his father proud.

Harvard Dunn tapped the last ream of documents together. "That concludes our meeting, gentlemen and ladies. I'm sure I speak for all of us when I wish Mr. Harper all the best."

"Thank you," Adam replied. "How is that project we talked about earlier coming along?"

Dunn glanced at him. "Project?"

"The wildlife refuge," Adam reminded him.

"That sounds intriguing," said a young female attorney with a come-hither smile.

"It's a place for animals injured in the wild to learn to readapt to their natural habitat," Adam explained. He didn't tell her he was building it for a certain mischievous coyote who was wreaking havoc at the Tate estate.

"I've already got the land purchase underway," Dunn informed him. "More than three thousand acres of pristine Wyoming rangeland. The next step—" The telephone at Adam's elbow buzzed.

"Excuse me for just a moment," he said, picking up the receiver. "Yes?"

"Adam? This is Katie."

His heart stopped beating for a moment. *Katie.* He hadn't seen her since that meeting in the Butte police station. He'd looked everywhere that day, frantic to find her. Eventually he'd learned she'd taken a flight to Grand Junction, Colorado. Dunn had informed him her family lived there and had wired her enough money to return home. Torn between chasing after her and giving her some time alone with her family, Adam had chosen the latter.

It had almost driven him crazy.

He'd picked up the telephone to call her at least a hundred times in the last two weeks, desperate to hear her voice again. But he'd never let the calls go through. He'd told himself to wait. Told himself to give her some time. She'd just regained her memory and barely survived a confrontation with Lorene and her gun.

If he had his way, they'd have the rest of their lives to spend together. In fact, he planned to formally ask her to do just that when he flew into Grand Junction tomorrow morning. Her phone call caught him completely off guard.

"Adam, are you there?"

"Yes. I'm here." He glanced up to see every suit in the room staring at him.

She hesitated. "How are you?"

"Fine." *Horrible. Rotten. Lonely. I miss you so much I can't stand it. I'm counting the hours until I can be with you again.*

"Good. I'm…fine, too."

"Good." He hated this stilted conversation, but he could hardly spill his heart out over the phone. Especially with several sharp-eared attorneys listening in. "Look, this really isn't a good time.…"

"I'm calling about Wiley," she interjected.

He blinked back his surprise. "Wiley?"

"I just wanted to check in and make sure he's all right."

"He's fine. He's still at Rodney's place."

"Oh. Good." Silence hovered on the line for a long moment. "I plan to go see him. I'm leaving today for Lightning Creek, then I'll head up to Montana.''

"Fine." *Perfect. Wonderful.* He'd be on the next plane to Butte.

"Well, take of yourself, Adam. Goodbye.''

"Katie, wait, I..." His voice trailed off as he heard the dial tone in his ear.

He'd blown it. Instead of sweeping her off her feet, he'd sounded as if he was just giving her the brush-off. Quickly he dialed the Lansing family number in Grand Junction, a number he'd memorized by heart. Then, before the first ring, he changed his mind and hung up the receiver. He still had a room stuffed with lawyers. Better to plead his case to Katie in person.

And he knew just how to do it.

CHAPTER FIFTEEN

"I STILL can't believe it," Marge said, holding a potted plant in her hands. "You had amnesia the whole time, and Katie O'Hara isn't even your real name."

"That's right." Katie shoved the last box of belongings into the back of her borrowed Jeep Wrangler. She'd come back to Lightning Creek one last time to gather the meager belongings from her small apartment above the Roadkill Grill. "Although my family used to call me Katie when I was a little girl. Maybe that's one reason the name appealed to me."

Marge clucked her tongue. "They must have been worried sick."

"They were," Katie confirmed, fondly remembering her reunion with them just one week ago. "When I hadn't called home for a while, they became concerned and contacted Baker and Dunn. But Lorene assured them I was fine and just out on assignment."

Marge's crimson mouth was pressed together in a thin line. "That woman should be horsewhipped after all the trouble she's caused."

"I don't think they horse-whip people anymore, but the state has filed charges against her for attempted bribery and aggravated assault."

"Serves her right," Marge grumbled, placing the potted plant in the Wrangler right next to the spare tire, "after what she put you through."

Katie leaned against the back bumper to catch her breath. "I just want to put it all behind me."

"Even Adam Harper?"

"Especially Adam Harper," Katie insisted, then marched toward the rickety metal stairs that led to her apartment.

Marge followed her, refusing to let the subject drop. "That man is worth a fortune. I'll bet all those buyers at the bachelor auction are kicking themselves that they let him go so cheaply. Impotent or not."

"You started the rumor," Katie said. "But for the rooord," she added on a soft sigh, "definitely not."

Marge raised a heavily drawn eyebrow. "Really?" She drew a notepad and pen out of her skirt pocket. "Now I have to hear the *whole* story."

A blush warmed Katie's cheeks. "I already told you the story, I just edited parts of it."

"All the good parts, it sounds like to me. Why'd you ever let him get away?"

To her chagrin, Katie's lower lip trembled. She bit it and took a deep breath. "It just…wasn't meant to be. I'd hoped Adam could forgive the fact that I'd lied to him and deceived him."

"With good reason," Marge said in Katie's defense.

"I assaulted him with a telephone and pilfered through his personnel files. Can you really blame him for not wanting anything more to do with me?"

Marge tipped her chin. "The Katie O'Hara I knew would never give up so easily."

"I didn't," Katie admitted. "I called him at his office right before I left home to come here."

"And?" Marge prodded.

"And he was very…polite." Her voice broke on the last word.

"Men," Marge exclaimed in disgust.

Katie swiped at the one lone tear that dared to seep out of her eye. "I don't know what else I expected. We hadn't even known each other a week."

"Sometimes it takes less time than that to know you've found your soul mate. Unfortunately, sometimes that soul mate has a thick skull. Want me to pound on it for you?"

Katie gave a shaky laugh. "Thanks, but I need to work this one out myself."

Marge's eyes widened. "So you're not going to give up on him."

"Of course not." Katie squared her shoulders. "As Scarlett would say, 'Tomorrow is another day.' So I'm off to find work in Chicago. After all, in a city of three million people, we're bound to cross paths sooner or later."

Marge licked the tip of the pencil. "Wait a minute, I want to get that down."

Katie watched her scribble on the notepad. "Marge, what are you doing?"

She glanced up. "Didn't I tell you? I'm the new special correspondent for the Lightning Creek *Gazette*. And I'm betting this story will make the front page."

Katie smiled, wondering why it had taken so long

for the weekly newspaper to discover the most valuable news source in town. "Good for you." Then she took one last look around the tiny apartment. "Well, I guess it's time to go."

"Oh, not yet," Marge said, seating herself on the lumpy sofa that had come with the furnished apartment. She patted the cushion next to her. "I just need to ask you a few more questions for my story. It will only take a minute."

Thirty minutes later, Katie was heading southeast on Highway 93. Lightning Creek would always hold a special place in her heart. During those few brief months after the accident, it had been the only home she'd ever known. Marge and so many other friendly residents had welcomed her with open arms.

She cracked open her car window, letting the fresh, warm breeze sift through her hair. Wild sunflowers sprang up on both sides of the highway, and feathery clouds dotted the wide expanse of azure sky. It was the perfect day for new beginnings.

Then she heard somebody sneeze.

Katie slammed on the brakes, her heart pounding. But not with fear. She looked in her rearview mirror just in time to see a dark head pop up from the luggage area in the back. *Adam.*

She pulled to the side of the road, shifted into Park, then climbed out of the car, her legs like rubber.

"I don't think I'm cut out to be a contortionist," he moaned when she opened the back of the Jeep.

"Adam," she squeaked, still reeling at finding him packed away in the back of the car along with her luggage and houseplants. She hesitated, then asked the question she wanted to know—was almost afraid to know. "What are you doing here?"

He pulled himself to a sitting position, grimacing as he unwedged his long legs from around the spare tire. "Well, I've been trying to track you down, but you always seem to be just one step ahead of me. I wanted to tell you about Wiley."

Her hopes plummeted. "Wiley? What's wrong? Has something happened to him?"

"He's fine," Adam assured her. "In fact, I've decided to use some of my newfound inheritance to open a wildlife refuge for injured animals and pet coyotes. He'll have literally thousands of acres to cause as much trouble as possible."

She swallowed hard. "That's wonderful."

He smiled. "Just one of the perks of suddenly finding out you're a millionaire. Of course, I won't have access to the money until all the legalities are finalized, so I've decided to go on a vacation."

Now she was both disappointed and confused. "A vacation?"

He nodded. "That's right. I heard a rumor you were headed for Denver. I've always wanted to see Denver."

She folded her arms. "I'm not going to Denver."

"Where are you going?"

"Chicago."

He grinned. "I've always wanted to see Chicago."

She smiled in spite of herself. "Isn't that where you live?"

"Actually, it is. It also happens to be where all

the leggy redheads gather." He gazed into her eyes. "In case you didn't know, they're my weakness."

She swallowed hard, telling herself not to get her hopes up again, no matter how much his blue eyes twinkled. But despite all her admonitions, her pulse still skittered and her skin tingled. "Are you looking for one in particular?"

"As a matter of fact, I am." He hopped off the tailgate, standing to face her. "Her name is Katrina. Although she sometimes goes by Katie." He took a step closer to her. "Which name does she prefer?"

"Katie," she breathed.

"Katie," he echoed, her name a caress on his lips. Then he cleared his throat. "The problem is, Katie was suffering from amnesia when she gave me some information. Unfortunately, she forgot something very important."

Her breath caught in her throat. "What?"

Adam reached leisurely into his shirt pocket and pulled out a folded sheet of paper. "One of the ingredients in this recipe."

She blinked at him in disbelief, then took the paper out of his hand. It was the barbecue sauce recipe she'd hastily written after Adam had caught her snooping in Rodney's study.

Adam turned and grabbed a brown paper sack out of the back of the car. "I've already bought everything on the list," he said, opening the sack and pulling out several large cans of tomato sauce, an economy-size package of brown sugar, three bottles of Worcestershire sauce and several assorted spices.

Katie watched as he unloaded the items onto the

open tailgate. "It looks like you've got enough for a year's supply of barbecue sauce."

He shook his head. "Not a chance. I'm just hoping it will last the weekend. But something is still missing."

She consulted the list in her hand, comparing it to the assorted grocery items. "It's all here. In fact, you've got enough supplies to triple the recipe. What could possibly be missing?"

"You."

The recipe fluttered out of her hand. "Say that again."

He took a step closer to her, his hand cupping her cheek. She closed her eyes at the exquisite sensation of his broad, rough fingers on her skin. Her memory perfectly recalled how deftly those same hands had caressed and aroused her one breathtaking moonlit night.

"You're the missing ingredient to make this recipe complete." Then he snapped his fingers. "Wait a minute, something else is missing, too."

She opened her eyes to see him pull a hairnet out of his pocket. Laughter bubbled up inside her as she took it from him and tossed it over her shoulder. "No way. I'm never wearing one of those again."

He sighed. "Then will you wear this instead?" He reached into his other pocket and pulled out a small, square box of black velvet.

Katie's breath caught in her throat as he opened the box. An exquisite emerald surrounded by a circle of radiant diamonds was nestled inside. *"Oh, Adam."*

"You bid your way into my heart for a measly

forty-seven dollars and fifty-five cents. Now you're so priceless to me I never want to let you go." He drew her into his arms. "Will you marry me, Katrina Katie O'Hara Lansing?"

Her eyes blurred as she leaned into him for a soul-searing kiss. "Absolutely."

Adam slipped the ring on her finger. "Now my fantasy is complete." Then he kissed her again. A deep, erotic kiss that made her stomach flutter and her skin hot. As their mouths melded together, so did their hearts. In a moment of desperation, Katie had bid on Adam Harper to find her past.

Now he was her future.

After kissing her so thoroughly she never wanted to leave his arms again, Adam lifted his head and grinned. "You know what this means?"

Katie laughed as she pulled him closer, her heart full of love and her life now complete. "Time to break out the barbecue sauce!"

HEART OF THE WEST

continues with

RECLAIMING JAKE

by

Patricia Keelyn

Ali Kendrick can't seem to put the past behind her—a past that revolves around bachelor Jake Merrill. As teenagers, she and Jake had spent endless hours in each other's arms. Then he ran away, leaving her alone and pregnant. Now, Ali's got the chance to get Jake out of her system for good. But once Jake discovers he's got a daughter, will he be able to walk away again?

Available now

Here's a preview!

ALI WOKE SUDDENLY with a sense of foreboding.

She lay for a moment, trying to pinpoint what had awakened her and why she suddenly felt so uneasy. From the cabin came the usual night sounds, the low pop of a dying fire, the mechanical hum of the refrigerator, a mountain breeze brushing against the outside shutters. And there was the soft snore of the man lying beside her. She turned to look at him for a moment and smiled. She'd never slept with a man before, and it was a delicious feeling.

Still, the sense of something wrong overrode that warmth.

Easing herself out of Jake's arms, she rose and slipped on his shirt. It smelled of him and for a moment, it eased her anxiety. Quietly, she made her way to the front windows.

Dawn wasn't far off. The eastern sky held the first promise of day, and soon the creek would be shimmering with sparks of sunlight. The night had been worth all the risk, and she wondered where tomorrow would take them. Certainly, she had a few concerns about how making love would affect their relationship, and how Jake would react when he learned he had a daughter. But this odd sensation was something else entirely.

Something she couldn't make sense of.

"What is it, Ali?"

She turned toward Jake, who'd risen up on one arm from their nest on the floor. "No, don't get up," she said, and walked back to rejoin him.

As she sank to the floor next to him, he reached out and brushed her hair away from her cheek. "Do you regret last night? Is that it?"

For a moment, she didn't answer, distracted by this other niggling fear. Then she forced a smile and shook her head. "No." And she realized it was true. Nothing about this weekend had turned out as she planned, but she couldn't say that she regretted it either. She had her answers.

She bent forward and kissed him lightly. "No regrets."

Drawing her closer, he deepened the kiss.

It was time to tell him about Sam. She'd put it off long enough, and maybe this was what was bothering her. Her need to tell him about his daughter. "Jake, there's something I need to tell you."

He nipped at her mouth while he unbuttoned the shirt she wore. "Did you ask if you could borrow this?" He pushed aside the fabric, and the cool morning air struck her breasts. "Later," he whispered. "We'll talk later."

Ali sighed. "Later," she agreed, and wove her fingers in his hair.

They took their time slowly exploring each other. A gentle touch, a soft sigh, a murmured endearment and he slipped inside her, filling her with more than his body. She felt her heart open up to him, welcoming him. And she didn't fight it. She let him in, body, heart and soul. He took her up slowly to the brink, and then eased back before she fell over. She moaned his name and held onto him, wondering how she'd ever be able to let him go.

Afterward, they fell asleep again, and Ali forgot her fear. Until the phone rang, sharp and intruding, and she sat bolt upright, her heart pounding in her chest.

Jake must have sensed her fear, because he released her immediately.

Pulling on his shirt again, she scrambled for the phone. "Hello," she answered breathlessly.

"Ali?" It was her friend Gail, but the moment she said Ali's name, she broke into tears.

"Gail," Ali insisted, "what is it?" Her own voice had taken on a note of panic and she was vaguely aware of Jake coming to stand behind her.

"It's the kids, Ali," Gail managed to say. "They're missing."

Available in August from

JOAN ELLIOTT PICKART

A brand-new, longer-length book
in the bestselling series,

The **Baby Bet**

*Party
of Three*

He was a hard-boiled cop with a child in his care.
She was a woman in need of his protective embrace.
Together they were a family in the making....

*Available at your favorite retail outlet.
Only from Silhouette Books*

DON'T MISS OUT!

MONTANA MAVERICKS: BIG SKY GROOMS
Three brand-new historical stories about the Kincaids, Montana's most popular family

**RETURN TO WHITEHORN, MONTANA—
WHERE LEGENDS ARE BEGUN AND
LOVE LASTS FOREVER BENEATH THE BIG SKY....**

Available in August 2001

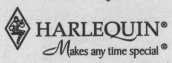

HARLEQUIN®
Makes any time special ®

Visit us at www.eHarlequin.com

PHBSGR

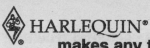